BOUNTY WAR

After the War Between the States, many small skirmishes still existed. A new governor, said to be a Yank, was in charge of the vast Arizona Territory and had branded as criminals the one hundred men led by Captain Murphy. Now these men were holed up in Dixiecity and had a two-hundred-dollar bounty placed on each.

When a trio of guerrillas stole into Pinetree, robbed the mercantile of ammunition, and absconded with three livery horses, Marshal Orion Tibbs was faced with a difficult situation.

He managed to kill two of the guerrillas but the third escaped. The bounty hunters knew that to attack Dixiecity head on would be dangerous with the winter snows packing in Crater Pass, so they began to devise a scheme to flush out the guerrillas. But Tibbs also had a plan, not only to bring the third guerrilla to trial, but also to aid Captain Murphy's men in a daring escape over the Mexican border . . .

BOUNTY WAR

A. A. Baker

GUNSMOKE

WESTERNS

First published 1972
by Avalon Books

This hardback edition 1992
by Chivers Press
by arrangement with
the author

ISBN 0 7451 4512 4

British Library Cataloguing in Publication Data available

Printed and bound in Great Britain by
Redwood Press Limited, Melksham, Wiltshire

Bounty War

1

Marshal Orion Tibbs eased the horse closer to the rim of Humboldt Shelf. Below, Pineville, Arizona Territory, squatted under black clouds. From this height it resembled a broken wheel. The four-story Palace Hotel was the hub; five blocks of business district were the spokes. The main street, wide enough for a Conestoga wagon to run without crossing the boardwalks, meandered down to a large cottonwood grove. The side streets, all very narrow and cluttered with decrepit buildings, faced out into mesquite-covered dunes.

Tibbs patted his horse and ruffled the mane. "Mick, Pineville always looks as if she's sitting right in the eye of a hurricane. Coming home, you never can tell if you'll get a hot bath or a slug in the back."

Mick arched his thick neck and bobbled his head until the bridle jingled. He was heavy in bone and deep of chest, both marks of a stayer. His eyes were large and wide apart. Mick had been mustered out of the cavalry; he was too intelligent and impatient of control. The army preferred animals who, like their troopers, learned by repetition and survived by instinct. Mick and the Marshal of Pineville made a good team.

Like an eagle approaching its nest, Tibbs scanned the wide valley. The water in the buffalo ponds rippled, and willows, growing out of the quagmire, bent under the increasing wind. A road snaked up the steep slope and clawed its rutty length into Crater Pass. The Pass was the only route over the Tooloon Mountains. When Tibbs glanced back, the peaks of the Tooloons disappeared in the storm clouds. South of those mountains lay Prescott, and then the flatland desert sloped all the way to Mexico.

Mick was impatient, but Orion studied the cottonwood grove. The Neston brothers had brought their cookwagon in a week ago. So far, fourteen rawhiders had joined, but Doc Neston was waiting for a large crew from Texas. The new governor—Orion spat—had placed a two-hundred-dollar bounty on every guerrilla brought in. Two hundred dollars was real money to the man hunters of the Southwest, especially because Captain Murphy's column of a hundred men were stranded at Dixiecity.

Tibbs glanced back at Crater Pass. One good

storm—and one was on its way—would plug up the Pass. Neston's reinforcements had better hurry. The snows would fill the lava gash and ice would drip from the crags. Pineville would be boxed in for the winter. He stirred uneasily, then clucked Mick into motion. "Let's get on down and see what's going on." The horse locked his front legs and slid over the rim.

Circling behind the hotel, Tibbs reined Mick toward Jeff Glory's livery stable. Its corral was empty. At the end of the alley sagged the Cantina, the oldest building in town and built by lazy hands. Tibbs, uneasy at the prevailing quiet, stiffened in the saddle. Mick's pointed ears flicked inquisitively.

As Tibbs passed the rear of Ben Bolt's mercantile store, the back door flew open, screen rattling. Mick shied. Three men, carrying rain sacks, erupted from the building. The lead man was Max Rosser from Dixiecity. He carried his gun in his hand and snapped a shot at Tibbs. The slug burned across Mick's withers, and the roan bunched and unwound. Tibbs, caught with one leg over the pommel, was thrown. He landed on his back, flipped around onto his elbow, and faced the three men.

Clawing out his Colt, Tibbs aimed and gave them their last chance. "Halt—right now!"

Bounty War

The bootheels continued to thump down the alley. Tibbs, aiming high, let off a round. Max Rosser returned the fire. His singing slugs kicked dust into Tibbs's face as the three men broke for the stable.

The marshal gained his feet as the men gained the safety of the barn entrance. Tibbs sped forward. At the double doorway he crouched next to a huge bougainvillaea and waited. When the three horses bolted from the barn, he was ready.

His first shot blasted a yellow-shirted man out of the saddle. The second horse, stumbling, crashed against the barn wall. The rider, raising his leg to avoid being crushed, turned to face the marshal. Tibbs shot him in the chest. The man's gun hand stiffened, and the horse raced out from under its dead rider.

The alley was filled with dust. Tibbs moved away from the bush. Max Rosser, flailing his horse with the sack, was leaving the alleyway. Tibbs fired a last forlorn shot. It missed and sang out into the dunes. Max Rosser skirted a walking dune and was gone. The two livery horses, led by a bucking Mick, were passing the Cantina and heading for open country.

Crossing the alley, Tibbs swiftly glanced at the pair of dead men, then hurried on into Ben Bolt's store. The proprietor was seated on the counter edge. Blood ran from a cut on his forehead, and he held himself erect by hooking an arm over a glass case.

"What in thunderation got into them?" Ben Bolt exploded.

Tibbs took a quick look around, then stepped behind the counter. The smell of fresh wood brought him to the back shelves. Cartridge boxes were ripped apart.

"That's all they come for and all they took," offered Ben Bolt. "Rimfire-tapered, copper-cased cartridges. Made special for navy Colts."

"Cavalry weapons," Tibbs muttered. He stepped back into the oil-stained aisle to take a closer look at Bolt's wound.

Angrily jerking away, Bolt demanded, "Ain't you going after them?"

"Only one got away. Two of them are dead. The other was Max Rosser and he's headed for Dixiecity. They were riding livery horses." Marshal Tibbs turned. "I'll step around and see how Jeff Glory made out."

The stable was dark and warm and, after the gunfire, almost eerie in the quality of its silence. Omar Clay had built this huge barn, and after he had died violently, Jeff Glory had taken over. Tibbs found Jeff at the work bench next to the tack room. He was propped against the bench, grimly fitting a new strap to his wooden leg. He greeted Tibbs with a shouted complaint.

"This old place could become a sticking pen or a graveyard, the way things are going wrong. Omar Clay was killed right where I'm standing. Gunned down by Gobel's gang. Now three of them Dixiecity guerrillas jam in and like to trample a man to death. They kicked me down, stole three of my best horses, and"—he shook the wooden leg angrily—"busted this danged strap!"

"Two of your horses are down the alley," Tibbs soothed the livery man. "Rosser rode off on the other one."

"Then why don't you go out and get him?" Jeff Glory demanded.

The marshal frowned. Ben Bolt, nursing his battered face, had asked the same question. It *was* an open-and-shut case of robbery and horse stealing, committed right in Pineville. A lawman should locate Mick and ride out on Rosser's trail. Tibbs studied that thought. A month ago there would have been no hesitation. That was before Judge Oleander Yontz returned from Prescott with new orders from the new governor. Dixiecity had been placed out of bounds for the Marshal of Pineville. The guerrilla hideout was to become the exclusive territory of Doc Neston's crew of deputized bounty hunters.

"Will you collect the bodies?" Tibbs fended.
"Omar Clay always handled the burials."

Jeff Glory fitted his stump onto the peg leg and
wrapped its strap securely before he answered. "I
buried my share of Rebs before they shot off my
leg at Ball's Bluff." He sidled up to the tall marshal and poked a thumb against his leather jacket.
"You got two bodies out in the alley? Ain't they
both guerrillas from Dixiecity? Ain't they worth
bounty?" His eyes lighted, and his breath quickened with hope.

"The poster says so," Tibbs acknowledged.
"Delivered in Prescott, they're worth two hundred dollars apiece."

Jeff Glory calmed himself to bargain. This
marshal had to be handled with kid gloves. He
was strung together with piano wire. Those cold
blue eyes looking out onto the world could turn
bleak or friendly; there was no in between. A man
never knew what was going on inside that long
head.

The livery man began to speak slowly. "Marshal, I was sure my luck had run plumb out.
Omar Clay's ghost haunts this stable. Last night
all my vines died. Today them three stole my
horses and busted my leg strap. Whyn't I just take
them two corpses and bury them down in Prescott?" Without waiting for an answer, he looked

up into Tibbs's set face and wailed, "Black cats don't run in front of me, they come down on my face when I'm sleeping!" He added, "A stomping horse never misses my good foot and—"

"Take them on in," Tibbs interrupted the petulant monologue. "Buy yourself a new peg. But you come back to Pineville, understand? Somebody's got to run this stable."

"Yes sirree, Marshal!" Jeff Glory spun jubilantly into the tack room and unhooked a set of buckboard harness.

The marshal walked the length of the barn, then stepped out into the alley. A small group looked up expectantly.

"Nobody's hurt," Tibbs reassured them. "Ben Bolt's head was cut and Jeff's strap was busted." He smiled softly. "Again."

"Then they made out better'n Wesley Neston," a dour man in a fur cap stated.

"So? What about Neston?"

"Them three caught him down at the Cantina," explained the trapper. "Max Rosser was wearing that sword-sash with a knot for every Yank he's killed." He waved toward Tibbs's victims. "With those two helping, Rosser corraled Wes Neston, took his weapons, hooked that sash around his neck, and strung him up on a rafter!"

2

The interior of the Cantina was dim. Un-washed windows collected cobwebs on the inside and dust on the outside. The dirt floor, packed solid, was stained by spilled drinks and tobacco juice. The low ceiling, once painted blue and red, was cracked and smoke-stained. Once a week the swamper swept with wet sawdust, cleaned the lamps, and scoured the tabletops. Carlos Gonzales and his seven sons served drinks, well-cooked meals, and dreadful guitar music.

A dozen men swarmed around Wesley Neston. He had been cut down, plied with mescal until he gasped for breath, and stretched out on a table.

Carlos Gonzales and Judge Oleander Yontz, both portly and gray-haired, turned as Marshal Tibbs entered.

"This *hijo, no es verdad, Senor* Tibbs, is very lucky, no?" Carlos waved his hands, stepped behind the bar, and asked, "Will you have something to drink, *Senor* Marshal?"

"Not now, Carlos." Judge Yontz directed the

marshal to the table. "Young Neston's lucky. One more jerk on that sash and he'd been in . . ." He paused, thought it out, and finished, "Wherever bounty hunters go."

Orion nodded and the judge went on: "This pup made a try for Max Rosser. All alone he tried to collect two hundred dollars of the governor's money. Max just wrapped that sash around his throat, and they hoisted him to the rafters and left him hanging."

"Senors, por favor," Carlos interrupted, "it is my pleasure to offer you something to drink?"

"Not now. Later on, maybe." Yontz was impatient.

"But, *senor*"—Carlos' eyes grew wet—"I am buying. It is on the house. It was not my fault. The young Neston, he is wearing the badge. The others . . . they were customers, no?"

"Nobody's blaming you, Carlos!" Yontz snapped. He whirled back to Tibbs and demanded, "What happened up there at the stable?"

Marshal Tibbs explained the brief fight and finished with, "Jeff Glory's taking them into Prescott for the bounty money."

Judge Yontz assumed a judicial frown. "You gave Jeff those bodies?"

"What bodies?" Wesley Neston, wiping at his face, rose from the table and gained his balance on unsteady legs. The younger Neston was a cull. His face was bloated and his wet hair straggled over his collar. He fumbled for his sweat-stained hat and tipped his head to glare up at the marshal. "You plug all three of them graybacks?"

Tibbs pushed against the sweaty shirt with a wide palm and shook his head. "Max Rosser rode off."

Wesley Neston flung his hat onto the floor and gave it a disgusted kick. "That's just glorious!" His voice was full of gall. "Old Doc's gonna be madder'n hell!"

Judge Yontz hooked an arm through Tibbs's elbow and led him over to the bar. He motioned for Carlos to pour. The white liquid gurgled from the bottle and spread out in the thick tumblers. Judge Yontz raised his drink and looked up into the marshal's face. "Orion, your very presence creates problems. You're a jackal or a hero. You must have been born to follow the roar of guns!"

Marshal Tibbs pushed back the tray Betsy Smith had sent over from the hotel. Cold coffee sloshed onto the desk, and Judge Yontz, glaring, reared back in his chair. "Watch what you're doing!" Like a wasp in a smokeout, Yontz was ready to sink his stinger.

They had been on the subject of Max Rosser

since leaving the Cantina. What had begun as a simple discussion had now become a full-scale battle of wills. Judge Yontz was insistent that it was Doc Neston's task to bring in Rosser. Tibbs felt strongly that the crimes had been committed in Pineville, so the local law should take precedence. The robbery at Ben Bolt's and the theft of Jeff Glory's horses had nothing to do with the Neston crew. Their commission was to hunt down guerrillas solely for crimes committed during the war. Tired of arguing, Orion Tibbs bluntly told Yontz that he intended to track Rosser into the Tooloons and bring him out.

The spilled coffee broke through Yontz's restraint, and he bellowed, "I'm tired of this discussion! I'm ordering you to leave every man in Captain Murphy's camp to the governor's deputies. Those are orders, Marshal!"

Orion Tibbs mopped at the spill. He had tried to handle the judge tactfully. Since his conference in Prescott with the new governor, Yontz had been moody. Captain Murphy's column were soldiers. Yet a carpetbagger of a governor had proclaimed them criminals. If caught by Doc Neston, they would have no trial. There were a hundred soldiers from Missouri left high and dry when the armistice was signed by Lee at Appomattox. This part of Arizona territory had become an escape route. Colonel Gater Grey's brigade had scuttled for the Mexican border. Captain Murphy's column had been left behind to cover the retreat. Federal troops had driven them into the Tooloons. They had planted a pair of howitzers on the ledges and fought off their attackers. Like hornets, they had thrown up fortifications and waited for a chance to escape.

Then there had been a change of governors. The new administrator, even before unpacking his carpetbag, had placed a bounty on every man in Dixiecity and sent in Doc Neston's crew of bounty hunters. Judge Yontz couldn't quite stomach that sort of lynch law. Now, faced with one of those double-edged decisions, the judge had turned to anger for justification.

Tibbs knew now he should have caught Mick and ridden out after Rosser. Waiting to discuss it with the judge had soured the entire matter. Tibbs continued to mop at the coffee spill and allowed the silence to gather.

Oleander Yontz kept his face blank, but his brain was churning. This stubborn man was dangerous; very, very dangerous. And, Yontz brooded to himself, he's a creation of mine. I had him paroled from Yuma Prison, pinned a star on his chest, and told him to clean up Pineville. And he had done just that. Whenever his gun comes out, someone dies. Pineville enjoyed its peace, and Tibbs's parole had been replaced by a pardon. Then the serenity exploded when the new governor declared Captain Murphy's company wanted men. The territory might have lived with that, as the column would have broken up and drifted off. However, deputizing the bounty-hunting Neston had changed the picture. The guerrillas at Dixiecity had to remain a fighting force. Their salvation depended upon each other. The governor's strategy was a puzzle. Why bounty hunters? Troops were available. Had the governor brought his own hate of Southerners into Arizona? Did he want scalps?

A knock on the door broke the silent deadlock in the marshal's office. With scowling relief, Judge Yontz opened the door. Doc Neston, removing his wide-brimmed hat, ducked his head and stepped inside. His bulk crowded the small office. Neston replaced his hat and towered above the judge. The governor's badge, a seven-point star, dangled from his soot-stained rawhide jacket. His own authority, two holstered Colts, brushed the buckskin fringe of his Texas chaps. Leather cuffs, seldom worn this far north, covered his thick wrists. He started cleaning his nails with a toothpick.

"Wes said you gave two dead Rebels to the liveryman for bounty." Doc Neston ignored

Judge Yontz and directed his statement to the marshal. He waited for Tibbs's nod, then went on, "My commission is clear and it's in writing, signed by the governor."

Tibbs considered carefully. "Well, *my* commission is to prevent crime or to bring in the criminals. Those two aren't dead *Rebels;* they're dead holdup men." He caught an appreciative glance from Judge Yontz.

Doc Neston ignored the distinction and spoke with condescension. "You done your job. An' seeing as how the liveryman's already got them bodies outta town, I'm letting him go. But I come by to warn you against crossing my trail again. Understand?" He made his threat, then passed on more information. "Soon as the rest of my men come in from Texas, we're rousting every Rebel cutthroat who's hiding out in your mountains."

To Tibbs's surprise, it was the judge who made an instant response. Yontz pushed his paunchy frame against the giant figure of Neston and snapped, "If Wesley Neston had been able to handle Max Rosser, the Marshal wouldn't've crossed your trail!"

"Wes just *let* him get the jump." Doc Neston brushed the words off, but blood flooded his face. "Anyway," he added, "there were three of them at the Cantina."

"There's a hundred at Dixiecity!" Yontz was ironic. "But what's a hundred to the Marshal?" The irony had turned to sarcasm, and, sputtering, he shrugged and wearily reseated himself.

Doc Neston gave Tibbs a look of mingled pity and respect. "If Tibbs goes into Dixiecity, he'll come out as cold as a frost-bitten chunk."

"You got any better in Texas?" challenged Yontz. Another thought struck him, and he waspishly added another question. "Where were you when Tibbs was fighting it out in the alley?"

Ignoring the challenge, Doc answered easily, "Scouting the hills." He turned away from the feisty judge and regarded Tibbs. "How many deputies you got?"

"We've got two." The judge refused to be ignored. "Both are out of town. Sid Peel's investigating rustling from Piper Garfield's spread. Fish-hunter's scouting a renegade bunch of Apaches from up north."

Neston accepted the judge's information without comment. "You sure enough going in alone?" he asked Tibbs.

"How's Wesley?" Tibbs parried.

The change of subject eased the tension. "Fool kid. He should've known Max Rosser hates Yanks," complained Doc Neston.

This was too much for Judge Yontz. He

jumped up quickly and demanded, "Wesley Neston? He's a Yankee? From *Texas?*"

Yontz's jack-in-the-box attacks dismayed the man hunter. He laid a hand on a gun butt, caught Tibbs's narrowing eyes, and instantly withdrew his tensed hand. "All the Nestons was for the South," he stated. "The governor, he's a Yankee. With us working for the governor, I suppose Rosser might feel we was Yanks, understand?"

"Anything for bounty!" Yontz sneered. He and Tibbs both wore an expression of disgust.

Confused, Doc Neston raised his voice. "You just get on up to Dixiecity, Tibbs, and get yourself killed! Soon as my men get here, we'll come on up and bring out your carcass!" Neston ducked his head, passed through the door, and the echo of his angry bootheels drifted back into the room.

"What a bullhead," croaked the judge, righting the spilled cup. "Better keep it all legal, Orion," he slowly added. "I'll give you a warrant for Max Rosser."

3

At dawn Orion Tibbs followed the frost-hardened ruts out of town. Jeff Glory's bougain-villaea, blooming yesterday, was now a frost-blackened stalk clinging to the wall of the barn. Leaving the Crater Pass road, he began working his way up the eastern slope of the Tooloons. The ice crystals, dangling from mesquite, tinkled as Mick brushed past.

As Pineville receded, Orion Tibbs had time to plan. Doc Neston's intrusion into the office confer-ence had riled the badgered Judge Yontz into switching his position. The warrant would give the marshal a legal right to invade Captain Mur-phy's camp.

Max Rosser, after spending a cold night on the trail, would arrive in Dixiecity about noon. He would report, and Captain Murphy would call in his subordinates. It was Tibb's guess that their de-cision would be to set up an ambush.

This was wild country. The mountains stood on end. Ridge stacked on ridge and canyons choked with sycamore, walnut, and wild cherry. Above the snowline manzanita grew shoulder-high, barricading the slopes and forcing invaders onto the exposed ridges. There were a thousand possible places to arrange a trap.

Dixiecity, flush against a lava flow, was a fortress in the sky. Bend Bow Canyon, crosscut by harsh winter torrents, had been plugged by slides. This meant one entrance and one exit. On a clear day sentries could spot visitors miles away. Tibbs inched up his sheepskin and was glad the snow was beginning to drift down. Larger flakes floated to gather on the foliage. If this storm lasted, the Nestons could collect all the bounty hunters in the West and still never overrun Dixiecity.

Tibbs knew a little about the guerrilla captain. Murphy had earned his commission on the firing line. Trained as a cannoneer during the Mexican War, Murphy had sharpened his skill against the Kansas Jayhawkers. The vicious border war had overlapped when the South seceded. With Lee's surrender, the Missouri guerrillas were outlawed and denied the right to take the oath. Colonel Gater Grey had salvaged a full brigade to seek safety in Mexico. Murphy had joined the flight. Colonel Grey, hard pressed by the Federals, had sent Captain Murphy's company into the Tooloons. The decoy had been effective and the brigade escaped into Mexico. Rumor had it that the former guerrilla commander was seeking a commission with Maximilian's army.

Captain Murphy proved a genius with his pair of mountain howitzers. In the maze of the Tooloons he had fought off the Federals. When the pursuit petered out, Captain Murphy had regrouped his force and fortified Bend Bow Canyon. With the stubborn conceit of soldiers refusing to admit defeat, they had named it Dixiecity.

Orion let his thoughts drift. Why had Captain Murphy lingered in the Tooloons? With the withdrawal of the Federal troops, he should have hurried south to rejoin Colonel Grey's command. Lack of horses, Tibbs guessed. That rugged retreat down from Missouri, ending the punishing fight in the mountains, would have exhausted man and horse. The men had recovered, but the horses . . . He shook his head in pity and gave Mick an affectionate pat on the neck. The horses had died. Mexico's border was close, but Captain Murphy's column was stranded. The Tooloons, once their salvation, had become their trap.

Orion Tibbs saw the black rifle barrel an instant before it spat out the screaming slug. He flung himself sideways. The manzanita prongs tore at his clothes, but he flailed deeper into the maze of scaly boughs. A second slug clipped the leaves, and he recognized the bark of a Spencer Carbine. Mick, quivering, had stood his ground.

The earth under the bushes, covered by layers of prickly leaves, crunched as Tibbs scraped around until he found a lichen-covered rock. He raised it swiftly and threw it. The rock caught Mick behind the stirrup. Shoes scraping on stone, Mick turned and obediently headed back toward Pineville.

Tibbs had caught one fleeting glance of Rosser's face behind the puff of gunpowder. Protecting his backtrail, the wily guerrilla had lain on this frozen slope all night. Relieved, Tibbs worked forward. Taking Rosser out here alone would be easier than from the guerrilla fortress.

Rosser had the high ground. He would have to be flanked and brought into the range of Orion's Colt. Keeping to the tangled undergrowth, Tibbs crawled forward. He listened. There was no creaking of brittle branches, no heavy breathing. Apparently Max Rosser knew how to play this game.

Twisted into swirls by the rising wind, the snow had increased. Fist-sized rocks, broken from weathered shale ledges, bruised Tibbs's hands. Pine snags lay under the packed leaves. After an hour of stalking, Tibbs placed his hat on a stick and held it above the manzanita. Nothing happened. No slug, no carbine report. He freed a rock from the decayed vegetation and chucked it upward. The wind moaned on and snow trickled silently down. Warily, gun drawn, Tibbs stood up. The silence was broken only by the wind.

Marshal Tibbs forced his way back to the trail. Snowdrifts covered the rocks. Had Rosser simply backed off and continued to Dixiecity? That wasn't too logical. Moving off the open trail, Tibbs located a shelf and crawled out of the weather.

Just how badly did Rosser want to kill him? The question nagged at his mind. Rosser had seen two of his comrades blown out of the saddle behind the livery stable. He knew that pursuit would develop. Would he pin down that pursuit for a single hour and then retreat to Dixiecity? Tibbs didn't think so. A man like Rosser would resent being chased down like a coyote. He would wait in ambush or—Orion smiled thinly—set another trap.

A hundred yards farther on he found where Rosser had ridden his horse back onto the trail. A few minutes later the hoof prints disappeared. Orion circled. Rosser had led his animal across some windblown rocks, reversed, then worked his way down. He wanted a victim pretty badly. He had thought like a fox, circling, now laying in a second ambush below. Well, Tibbs wasn't about to trip the jaws of the trap twice. Rosser had assumed that his victim, horseless, would try to get down out of the storm. Only a fool would go higher. Hoping Max Rosser would freeze while waiting, Orion continued upward. He had a few hours of daylight left. He would find a place to hide and catch Rosser when he came on.

Max Rosser would soon guess that his victim had gone ahead. The horse he had stolen, fattened in Jeff Glory's stables, would be rested. Once Rosser decided to head for Dixiecity, he would come on fast.

The scrub brush dropped behind Orion. A trail followed the ridge. An increasing wind swept away the clogging snow, and drifts, piled against ledges, were snatched apart and floated out into the canyons.

Max Rosser would come this way, and soon. A horseman would be facing the wind, his head down, body hunched. He would never expect a man to drop aboard from above.

Orion's slicker had gone with Mick. He drew his jacket close and tied a bandana over his hat. He could hold out for another hour. Then he would have to locate a hideout and hole up until the storm blew itself out.

Rounding a mound of rocks shaped like shale stairs, he climbed up and crouched in a widened crack. As he waited, an intense blast of wind suddenly cleared a view. Above him, like a frosted castle, loomed Dixiecity. A sentry tower, plastered with snow, rose above gates of sharpened stakes. The walls were high, but from his rock mound Orion could make out the sloping roofs of long barracks. The wall of rock gave them some protective cover.

Captain Murphy had chosen his site, fortified it, and would be reasonably safe from attack. Orion guessed they had a water supply but doubted that they had a source of food. Snipers, located along the ridge, could take the spirit out of attackers. The lightweight howitzers would protect the sniper's withdrawal and smash any grouping invaders. A charge would be crushed by a crossfire from the walls. This place could be taken only by siege and the help of cannon. Doc Neston certainly didn't plan to storm this fort. The wily bounty hunter might be able to starve this garrison out or—Orion shrugged his thinking away. It wasn't his concern.

He shivered in his crevice. The hour went slowly by. Dusk eased in under the relentless snowfall. Had he guessed wrong? Max Rosser had a good horse. Wasn't it likely that he had ridden back into the lowlands to wait out the storm? He might also attempt Crater Pass and try to reach the Mexican border.

A hunched rider in a black hat, like a floating ghost, appeared in the snowfall. Rosser had his arms tucked under a thin coat. Orion guessed a folded fist gripped the butt of a navy Colt.

Orion leaned out and tossed a rope, successfully pinning Rosser's arms. In the struggle the double weight overbalanced the horse and it stumbled. Rosser freed his gun and fired. Before he could trigger a second shot, Tibbs raised his own Colt and knocked the weapon out of the guerrilla's hand. He kicked at Rosser's right stirrup and knocked the boot loose. Then he leaned hard. Rosser was going over and made a grab for the pommel. The horse bolted. Rosser's bootheel had slipped through, and now he was being dragged. Spooked, the horse tried to outrun its burden. Tibbs staggered along, snatching at the dragging reins.

A flash of gunfire erupted from the sentry tower. "Stand right where you are!" a grim voice ordered. "Take one more step and you're a dead man!"

Tibbs froze. The stockade gate swung outward. A man flung his full weight onto the horse's head and dogged it. Straddle-legged, the horse was

snubbed to a halt. Max Rosser was lifted to his
feet and led inside.

A sergeant tramped through the gates to confront Tibbs. Peering close, he demanded, "Just
who in blazes are you?" He was bundled in a coat
that fell to his boot tops. Snowflakes caught in his
black beard, and his breath vaporized in the cold
air. Altogether he was a picture of a starved and
weary man.

"Name's Tibbs. I'm the marshal of Pineville."

"Figured you for a Neston," growled the sergeant, who reached out and grabbed Orion's arm,
then marched him toward the gate. As they passed
the sentry tower, the sergeant shouted, "Come on
down here!"

When the sentry stepped off the ladder, the sergeant snatched the carbine from him and shouted,
"Someday you'll learn!" He triggered a shot,
ejected the casing, then fired once more. "Orders
were to fire twice for an alert!" With a force that
brought a grunt from the sentry, he shoved the
weapon back into the man's hands. Satisfied that
matters had been returned to a military footing,
he snapped at Tibbs:

"Now, Yank, you just march right on into
Captain Murphy's quarters."

4

Captain Murphy's headquarters consisted of a single huge room. Barked but unsquared beams supported the roof. This was a redoubt of rugged construction. If the outer gate were ever breached, many would die against these heavy walls. The place smelled of warm horseflesh, almost as strong as Jeff Glory's stables. In the dim light from the fireplace Tibbs could see that the room was divided by a waist-high railing. Behind the railing he counted twelve horses. On the near side living and office quarters were combined.

The sergeant caught Tibbs's inspection and remarked, "We don't leave our horses out in the weather." He pulled at his beard, then added, "What horses we have."

The captain had risen from a table near the fire and stood waiting. His knee-length cavalry boots were scarred but polished. The gray uniform was patched at the elbows and cuffs with black leather. Where the lining showed, it was stained and worn. He wore a collar insignia of crossed cannons. Captain Murphy was a heavy man with wide shoulders and a barrel torso. Tibbs could envision him cradling a mountain gun on a lumbering run. Stalking forward now, the officer reminded Tibbs of a bulldog braced to fight.

Even though his uniform was shabby and his quarters part stable, Captain Murphy was impressive. He would have to be a professional officer, Tibbs thought, to hold a crew of guerrillas together in this wild back country.

"Wait outside, Sergeant." Murphy's voice was a tone higher than expected. It was modulated, Tibbs thought, to break through the sounds of battle.

He indicated the glowing fire. "Warm yourself, mister. I understand you're a law officer?"

"District Marshal." Tibbs lifted the warrant from his shirt pocket and smoothed it. "A warrant for one of your men, Max Rosser."

"Very unusual, a town marshal following a man into these mountains. This is well out of your jurisdiction. Your authority is no good here."

Tibbs lowered his head stubbornly. He recognized the deft circling of the military mind. "This warrant was issued by a federal judge. As for my jurisdiction, it extends as far as is necessary. Especially when a crime has been committed in Pineville."

"Please explain the charges against Rosser." Captain Murphy ignored the warrant.

Briefly Tibbs related the details of the theft of Jeff Glory's horses and the robbery of Ben Bolt's store. He made no mention of the near lynching of Wesley Neston.

"And the two men with Rosser?" The captain was glowering.

"Both dead. Their bodies are on the way into Prescott," Tibbs evenly replied.

"For bounty?" Murphy's lips were a grim slit. "Four hundred dollars for two? That's a fair day's pay for a back-county marshal."

The marshal ignored the taunt. "They broke the law. Rosser will be returned to Pineville for trial."

"In Judge Yontz's court?" The question was openly sarcastic. Before Tibbs could answer, Captain Murphy pounded a fist into the palm of his hand. "Yontz is a henchman of the new territorial governor. A number-one bootlicker." His voice spluttered on. "We've been refused amnesty, denied the right to cross into Mexico. A bounty has been placed on every man in my command. Doc Neston's man hunters have been deputized. Add your charges of theft and horse stealing, and any trial in Pineville would be a complete farce. What sort of justice places a bounty on a soldier's life?"

"That's between you and the governor," Tibbs said simply. "Max Rosser is charged with stealing a horse and robbing a Pineville store. I'm taking him in."

"Not into a lynch court!" Captain Murphy shouted. He cast a speculative look around and forestalled an answer by raising a hand. "We know Doc Neston has established his camp in Pineville. With winter coming on, isn't that stupid? No one can get at us until the spring."

Tibbs wished the man would stick to one track. Murphy kept linking Doc Neston's mission to the arrest of Max Rosser. He was pressing for information that Tibbs could only guess about. Doc Neston was a professional man hunter. He would never attack this fortress in the winter, nor would he gather a crew to wait until spring. Obviously Captain Murphy was in trouble. He needed ammunition, but, even more important, he needed horses. Twelve horses for a hundred men. Dejected, weary animals, hardly fit to pull a buggy. Slaughtered and salted, they just might provide enough food for a marchout. Certainly they would never feed this column for the winter. There was something shaping up. A reason for Doc Neston to require a strong force immediately.

"Doc Neston works for the governor," Tibbs said. The job at hand was to get Rosser out of this place and into Judge Yontz's courtroom. What happened, or was about to happen, between Doc Neston and Captain Murphy was beyond Tibbs's control. "Rosser's crimes were against citizens of Pineville. That *is* under my jurisdiction. You have my warrant, Captain. Turn him over to me."

Captain Murphy, like a sniper sighting, lowered an eyelid and spoke flatly. "We have been refused our rights by your government, so we reject your laws." His lip curled as he raised his voice. "Sergeant of the Guard!"

Boots crunched in the snow and the door flew open. The sergeant appeared, a lumpy figure in the opening. "Yes, sir, Captain?"

"Lock this man up!"

"But, sir, Max Rosser is in there."

"Release him and bring him here." Murphy turned as Tibbs was led out. To himself he muttered, "Would we had more like *him!*"

A narrow parade ground separated the barracks from the headquarters building. Their steep roofs slanted away from the overhang of the cliff. The walls of peeled logs were mortared with clay; the doors were wide and hinged with bullhide. The windows were made of squares cut from shelter tents. The guerrillas had built Dixiecity to last.

Each building had its own chimney of sticks

plastered with thick mud. Firelight glinted from the smoky stacks and seeped out of the windows. The faint light outside outlined an empty corral and very sparse wood piles. Tibbs sensed a moodiness about the place. Captain Murphy had been worried. Had the storm interrupted a breakout? Or had Doc Neston's arrival interfered?

Orion Tibbs spent the long hours before midnight pacing the eight-by-ten-foot cell. The dirt floor, muddied by the new snow blown under the sill and through the barred grill, had turned icy.

The jail sentry, his lean face sprouting straggly whiskers, was a chilled young private. His eyes were sunken, and his large Adam's apple protruded against his whiskery neck. The camp slept while the private maintained his lonely pacing.

Waiting until the sentry was near and would hear, Tibbs raised a knee and jammed his bootheel into the clay. It broke. Wind whistled in and he kicked again. The wall shook.

"What's going on in there?" The guard had moved to the barred opening. He held a rifle in cold hands covered by tattered mittens. Buckled around his shabby greatcoat was a holstered navy Colt. He moved closer to the opening and, eyes rolling, glared in.

Moving forward, Tibbs began searching his shirt pocket. "Guess your jailhouse was built right. Say, I got the tobacco and papers; you got matches?"

"You got real tobacco, sure enough?"

Orion displayed the sack, and the sentry's avid eyes followed the bag. He raised a thin hand. Tibbs withdrew the tobacco sack a full six inches. Eyes fastened on the sack, fingers extended, the sentry worked his hand past the bars. It took but a second for Orion to reach out, grab the nape of the thin neck, and yank the sad face against the cold bars.

"One peep out of you and I'll break your neck!" Orion gritted. "Now pass in that Colt!" With his clutching arm he jerked a firm warning. The bugged eyes blinked assent and the butt of the pistol was pushed inside. In moments the bar was raised and the sentry hauled inside and bound.

Tibbs stayed close to the shadows, circled the parade grounds, then halted at the wall of Captain Murphy's headquarters. He listened and heard the stomp of the restless horses. Opening the door a crack, he could see the interior dimly lighted by the flames flickering on the hearth. Max Rosser was sprawled on a skin next to the fire. Captain Murphy had hung his coat over a chair farther inside. The twenty brass buttons glinted. Murphy, his face to the wall, was asleep in a bunk. Tibbs entered and crossed the cold stone floor to the railing.

Jeff Glory's horse was cribbing the halter railing. It was the one decent animal present. Tibbs had been quite right. This was a desperate, worried column. These mounts were stabled in this building much as hogs being held in a slaughter pen. Were they to be meat on the hoof while the Missouri guerrillas hiked for Mexico? Then why had they delayed? Orion dropped the problem. He was after Max Rosser. Amnesty and bounties were the governor's problems. Orion moved quickly to the bunk and hooked a hand into Captain Murphy's undershirt. When the captain opened his eyes, he was staring into the barrel of the navy colt.

"Keep quiet, Captain," Tibbs ordered. He raised the man and led him across the room. Max Rosser turned over. Tibbs stepped to one side and roused Rosser with the toe of his boot. Captain Murphy, shivering, stood stoically as Orion disarmed his second captive.

Nudging the officer with the gun barrel, Orion stated, "I'm taking Rosser out. You both get your clothes on, then saddle three horses."

Captain Murphy's shaggy head came up and his chin squared. "I'm not leaving!" he stated, low and evenly.

The silence gathered. Tibbs had the upper

hand but only inside this building. The Rebel captain, his pride damaged, was man enough to take a slug before he would be marched off.

With the weapons available, Tibbs might hold out for a few hours. He looked around. The howitzers, polished and oiled, were positioned against a side wall. Wooden boxes, banded with brass, held the howitzer shells. His captive's eyes followed his look.

"I can spike those guns," Tibbs said coldly.

"So?" Murphy moved as though to pace, reconsidered, and frowned. Max Rosser, taut as a mountain cat, was gathering his lean strength.

Orion threw out a guess. "You fought off the Federals once. Now Doc Neston is gathering men. Without those cannon"—he flicked a hand toward the horses—"and nothing to ride, can you do it again?"

"You'd condemn a hundred men?" Murphy was bitter.

Orion Tibbs shook his head. "You're the one who will be doing that, Captain."

"You'd never get out alive!"

Orion gave some thought to the threat, then, pointing his Colt at the ammunition boxes, stated, "I might."

The room was stuffy with tension. Captain Murphy knew this marshal wasn't bluffing. One

move and that gun would bark. Tibbs recognized
the captain's predicament. The loss of those field
pieces meant that his command would be sliced
up. The Nestons, or the army, would hunt down
and kill the men Murphy had led all the way from
Missouri. Men who had followed him through a
hundred campaigns. Should they now be butchered? Rosser was one soldier. A soldier to be mar-
tyred for a column?

Max Rosser broke the stalemate. "It's a
Mexican standoff. I'll break it, Captain. I'll go in
with the marshal. But only providing it's just him
and me." Rosser's lips raised in a stiff grimace. He
faced Tibbs, and his black eyes snapped. "Understand that, Yank?"

Tibbs nodded. The captain's head drooped.
Reassuringly Max Rosser chattered on. "Won't be
no trouble, Captain. All they got me for is horse
stealing and lifting a tote sack full of cartridges."
He chuckled, almost gravely. "Besides, how's this
Yank marshal know he can get me in there?" He
accepted Captain Murphy's silence as assent and
broke the spell by moving over to the horses.

Tibbs tensed for Captain Murphy's decision.
Rosser's involuntary submission had been a surprise. The captain slowly nodded, and Orion's
suspicions grew.

"You've got your deal, Marshal." The captain

was scowling. "Get saddled up. I'll pass you through." He stepped up to Tibbs. He was a full head shorter, but he swelled with anger. "One thing more, Tibbs. If anyone takes Rosser in for bounty, you'll die for it! You think about that, Marshal!"

Orion Tibbs nodded and walked stiffly to the horse pen. This was a grim game they were playing. Law and order were pushed aside. Captain Murphy had made his threat as a man who would back it up. Vaguely Orion Tibbs suspected that protecting Max Rosser was going to be more difficult than bringing him out of Dixiecity.

5

Judge Oleander Yontz had moved his cane-bottomed chair to the end of the Palace Hotel's porch to avoid the cold wind. Below, on the first step, Fish-hunter whetted the shining blade of his bowie knife. Betsy Smith, wearing a gingham dress covered by a voluminous apron, rocked slowly while she shelled peas.

"But it's already been two days since Mick came home!" exploded the judge. "I know just what you're going to say. 'Tibbs can take care of himself.' It isn't the marshal I'm worrying about. It's how many has *he* killed!"

Betsy laughed heartily, and Fish-hunter stifled a grin. Since Orion Tibbs had left on Max Rosser's trail, the judge had grown increasingly irritable. Mick's return had only heated the judge's temper.

"Don't you laugh." Yontz held up one finger and then arced it toward the ground. "Tibbs is needed right here. His job is taking care of

Pineville. With Neston's bounty hunters gathering, we could have a calamity erupt!"

"Calamities happen, volcanos erupt," soothed Betsy. She brushed back her dark locks and curled the ends around her fingers. "Don't you forget, Judge, those bounty hunters were sent in here by the new governor. And," she tartly added, "the war is over. The last battle has been fought. Those Dixiecity men fought for their side, so why should they be hunted down?"

"Fought? Pshaw!" snapped the judge. "Murdered and looted are what they did. That Max Rosser—doesn't he have fifty-four knots on his saber-sash? One knot for every Yank he's killed?"

"Only fifty-four?" Betsy mewed. "Doc Neston has killed a hundred men."

"His were mostly Apaches," Yontz retorted.

"You speak only of the number each man has killed?" Fish-hunter was mildly reproving. "If Max Rosser killed fifty-four men and is then killed by Marshal Tibbs, can't Tibbs claim a total of fifty-five?"

Yontz, openly hostile, sneered. "If he lives, Tibbs will beat them both."

Laughing, Betsy Smith winked at Fish-hunter. She halted her teasing then to ask soberly, "You really are concerned about Orion, aren't you, Judge?"

He ignored her and ranted on. "And that poor dumb Jeff Glory, starting out in a snowstorm. Bounty money breeds greed. It might be fine down on the border, where the Apaches and the Yaqui have to be brought under control, but bounty hunting the guerrillas could push this territory into a civil war!"

"Thank you, no, we've just had one!" Betsy rose, tucking her collander under her elbow as she marched into the hotel.

"And where's Sid Peel?" Yontz was hitting out in all directions. "Just where is that bandy-legged shadow? Out trailing Tibbs?"

Fish-hunter rose and sheathed his bowie. "Sid has gone to see Piper Garfield. Garfield has complained of butchered cattle."

Yontz growled at the information. "Everyone knows Piper moved his cattle out of the Tooloons weeks ago. You know he scatters them out on the flatland for winter grazing. Then he takes off for his winter spree. Sid will get locked out on the far side of Crater Pass. Finding Garfield will be like locating a ghost in a fogbank."

Fish-hunter had had enough. This was one of Judge Yontz's unstable days. Everything was going wrong. Yontz liked to make his decisions on strict, legal lines. Max Rosser's exploit had thrown him off the track. Now the judge was faced with holding court on a man charged with normal crimes, in addition to being on the wrong side in a civil war.

"Where you going?" he demanded as Fish-hunter strode out into the street.

"To open the jail."

"Eh?"

"Judge, if you will look down the road, you will see that Marshal Tibbs is returning. He has a prisoner, and it is only natural I have a cell ready." Shaking his head and hoping that Tibbs could calm down the judge, Fish-hunter crossed the street to the marshal's office

Judge Yontz leaned out to look. No one could fail to recognize Marshal Tibbs. He sat tall on a horse. He carried his head high and exuded a springlike strength. Tibbs was a coiled frame of rawhide and wire, mused Yontz; a coiled spring leaping out just the required distance. Yontz sighed and muttered defensively to Fish-hunter's retreating back, "Well, his job *is* here."

The man riding behind Tibbs would be Max Rosser. Yontz looked again, grumbling. That would set off the fuse in the powder barrel. He glanced toward the grove. Doc Neston's camp had been growing. Before the storm blocked Crater

Pass, fourteen more gunslingers had arrived. Yontz hated to guess the number still south of the pass, waiting for it to reopen.

During the days of Tibbs's absence, Yontz had gotten the full story of Max Rosser's fracas with Wesley Neston. Wesley had drawn his gun. The kid was excited and trying for the capture of a guerrilla. Max Rosser had tipped the kid off his bar stool, looped that yellow sash around his neck, and hoisted him to the rafters. The three guerrillas had taken time to loot Ben Bolt's cartridge bin and to steal Jeff Glory's horses. Well, two of them were dead, and the third man was being brought in right now.

Orion Tibbs and his prisoner approached the hotel. Yontz noted that Fish-hunter had already appeared in the doorway of the marshal's office, holding a vicious four-barreled shotgun. Omar Clay, before his death, had made a pair just for the marshal. The revolving breech triggered like a handgun. Lord, Yontz gritted, what a town to live in! Every day it moved a few feet closer to Hades. The grove was filling up with man hunters. Tibbs, who only pulled his gun to kill, had returned. Fish-hunter, an educated Indian, would walk into a nest of wildcats on Tibbs's orders, and there was Sid Peel, a spider of a man who was lightning with a gun. And where was Sid? Searching for Piper Garfield? That was part of the trouble with Pineville's law officers. No one took the time to inform the judicial branch. It was simply run them down or outgun the lawbreakers. Dang it all, he thought angrily, they still have to be tried.

Yontz sniffed. Betsy Smith was stoking up the stove to fry Tibbs a platter of antelope steaks. Always the same. She seemed to sense when he would return. Intuition? Yontz rose and stalked across the hotel porch. By Harry, that was something he could use, a crystal ball!

Nodding as he passed the judge, Tibbs guided his horse across to the jail. Max Rosser, following with bound hands, threw the judge a wink. Fishhunter prodded the prisoner down and inside to lock him up.

Orion Tibbs poked the coals alive in the round-topped stove. He reached into the low rafters and brought down a second Omar Clay Special, another four-barreled shotgun. In the back, the cell door clanked, and Fish-hunter entered the small office.

Removing a swab from the short barrel, Orion looked up to ask, "How many down at Doc Neston's camp?"

"Some got over the pass before the heavy snow," Fish-hunter replied. "All told, there's about fourteen down in the grove."

"Sid could be caught up there in the pass," Orion speculated. "And Jeff Glory." He smiled with his eyes. "I'd say Jeff is snowed in. No buckboard could make it." They both grinned at the thought of the volatile stableman snowed in with a pair of corpses.

"What's so funny?" Judge Yontz was standing in the doorway. He made a half fist to point with his thumb at the brutal weapons held by the officers. "Enjoying the thought of blowing somebody apart? One of the Nestons, maybe?"

"Just getting ready, Judge," Tibbs answered without rancor. "Neston men are arriving, right?" He waited for Yontz's stiff nod, then added in a flat, hard voice, "Nobody's going to take Max Rosser out of this jail."

"For bounty they might try!" Yontz was still angry.

"He's charged with robbing a store and stealing three horses." Orion tried to keep it all simple. "You made out the warrant. It was for robbing a store and—"

"Stealing the horses!" rasped Yontz. "*I* know what it was for! But the Nestons *are* deputized and—"

"Not by me they aren't." Orion calmly broke down the shotgun to grease the cylinder.

"You're just bullheaded!" snapped Yontz. He realized that Max Rosser had committed his crimes in Pineville, and so the town marshal brought him in; yet couldn't Tibbs turn Rosser over to the Nestons? Exact an agreement that they, in turn, would transport Rosser into Prescott?

Orion ignored Yontz's remark. "You try him, Judge. If he's found guilty, I'll transport him to the territorial prison at Yuma."

"They'll try to take him," Yontz warned.

Orion patted his gun and answered coldly, "If they do, the governor'll need to deputize more man hunters."

Yontz winced. The words weren't a threat, simply a cold statement of fact. A clash between the Nestons and this pair of lawmen would strew the streets of Pineville with casualties. The four-barreled weapons didn't reach out far, but buckshot raised havoc at short range.

"Give me two hours." Yontz wearily accepted Tibbs's ultimatum. "Court will convene in the parlor of the hotel." With a stiff back and clenched fists, Yontz waddled back to the hotel.

6

The trial of Max Rosser promised to be a grand event for Pineville. It had been a dull summer. Renegade Apaches had slithered out of the Francisco desert, been caught and hung. There had been one minor engagement between the buffalo hunters and the Garfield cowboys. Captain Murphy's running fight with Federal cavalry had ranged through the higher mountains, away from Pineville. Isolated from the rest of the territory by mountains, almost swallowed by sand and endless horizons, Pineville craved excitement.

Marshal Tibbs's expertise with the handgun had kept crime to a minimum. Hard cases, drifting in to look for trouble, had quickly found that such a path ended at the cemetery. Even Piper Garfield's brushpoppers had learned to control their behavior while in town.

The arrival of the Neston crew had sparked some awe and much speculation. Doc had a reputation. He swaggered on the thin rim of the law. Preferring to take his head money off a dead body,

Doc, when pushed, could stand up to the best with bare fists, bowie, or Colt. The difference between Marshal Tibbs and Doc Neston was razor-thin. Doc killed for money, Tibbs to enforce the law. The same type of man, but two kinds of law.

There had to be a showdown, and the citizens of Pineville now believed the trial of Max Rosser could spark it. As for Rosser's chances, the permanent bartender at the Palace, Barnaby Able, put it all in a nutshell. Rosser was as good as dead already. He had killed fifty-four men. "He's got no more time to borrow against. Holding him for trial is like sending out a posse to dig up a corpse. It's wasting a lot of time to bury him again." Barnaby swished his bar towel and nodded smugly. "Whatever happens at the trial, it ain't going to end up in no shivaree!"

Citizens agreed. The Neston brothers were as mean as mountain cats. Marshal Tibbs had already snatched two valuable bodies from their predatory claws. Max Rosser was number three for Tibbs. When the trial was over, Judge Yontz would have to sentence the guerrilla on both counts. Max Rosser would be an old man before he ever got out of Yuma Territorial Prison. So, good-bye bounty money for Doc Neston.

Barnaby Able poured drinks and added it all up. "She'll be a regular pit fight. Two pumas against a stubborn grizzly. And a pit dog for a judge."

When the time arrived, Judge Yontz's courtroom was jammed. The podium was a poker table set on the dais in one corner of the parlor. The room gradually filled with the smell of sheepskin coats, waxed boots, and strong tobacco. Doc and Wesley Neston, flanked by border gunslingers, found seats up front. Men lining the brocade-covered walls shifted their feet and talked in low voices.

During other trials it had been a more convivial atmosphere. Men had sidled in, glass in hand, from the bar. Hearty exchanges and a few bets would have raised a cheerful din. This was something different. Weapons had been checked in the anteroom. Fish-hunter, grave and brisk, patrolled the inner balcony. Every man in the room could feel those coppery eyes drill against his skull. They threw glances upward, then shifted uneasily, mentally dodging the black muzzles of the four-barreled shotgun.

The judge entered. As he moved up the aisle, men rose and the talk stilled. Yontz had spruced up. His frock coat showed marks of a firm brushing. His paper collar was fresh and circled by a black string tie. He reached the table, flipped his coattails to one side, then seated himself. Raising

the gavel, he caught Fish-hunter's eye and nodded. With forceful authority, he banged three
sharp raps to open court.

Doc Neston cynically eyed the assembly. Wesley
Neston, taut and strained, watched the door for
the prisoner's entrance. Several of the bounty
hunters exchanged looks, then lowered their eyes.

"Court is called to order," Yontz stated.

Marshal Tibbs and Max Rosser's bootheels
could be heard crossing the anteroom. Max Rosser entered the parlor ahead of Tibbs and paused
arrogantly. He locked eyes with Wesley Neston.
Tibbs jostled the prisoner's elbow and moved him
to a seat at the rear of the dais. All present stared
at Tibbs. His left elbow was curled about his
four-barreled shotgun. The palm of his right
hand caressed the hammers.

The room was filling with tension. Feeling it,
Yontz flicked a speculative frown over the crowd.
He put some of his concern into his opening
words. "Let it be known that this courtroom is
heavily guarded. Anyone daring to intimidate this
court or harm the prisoner will be firmly handled.
Do I make myself clear?" A low murmur of assent
rose. Yontz nodded and banged the gavel for
order. Even as the hardwood slapped the table,
the uneasy quiet broke and Yontz looked up.

Wesley Neston had risen, taking two measured

steps into the aisle. His right arm was lifting. As his elbow bent, a two-shot derringer seemed to leap into his hand. Wesley Neston's face was a mask of hatred. One eye squinted while his mouth contorted into a snarl. Like a puppet, the judge acted on his reflexes, trying to move away from the path that the bullet was to take.

Marshal Tibbs drew his Colt and triggered the hammer. The explosion of the Colt and the crack of the derringer blended. Wesley Neston was knocked off balance by Tibbs's heavy slug. The Neston crew moved quickly to gather around the fallen man.

"Watch them!" Tibbs shouted to Fish-hunter and hurried toward Max Rosser. Doc Neston met him on the first step and butted the marshal aside. Tibbs swung the shotgun. Several other men had crowded in behind Neston and gathered around the prisoner's overturned chair. Tibbs, using the gun butt, wedged the group apart. Max had fallen forward. Tibbs raised his wobbly head and saw that Max's eyes were glazing and his thin lips freezing into a last, wry grimace.

Doc Neston swung around to face the marshal and shouted, "That varmint had a weapon!" He raised a hand above the milling men. Those on the dais steps parted, and Doc Neston was display-

ing a second derringer in his meaty hand. "This is
why Wesley made his move. He'd seen this!"

Doc Neston's roaring voice, the sight of the
handgun, and Tibbs's threshing with the gun
butt panicked the crowd. Chairs crashed and a
man cursed with pain. Like a headless glob, they
flowed toward the exit.

"Everybody calm down!" Fish-hunter shouted.
"Hold it right where you are!" The men in the
rear, trying to get a look at Max Rosser's body,
broke out in excited conversation. Judge Yontz
had recovered and was excitedly pounding with
his gavel. The crush toward the door continued,
and angry men flailed at each other.

Fish-hunter triggered a shot into the ceiling.
The heat from the blast and the smell of powder
brought calm out of confusion. As the men
quieted, chips of plaster and flakes of paint drifted
down.

Shoving men aside, Orion Tibbs pressed into
the aisle and bent over Wesley Neston. He was
badly hurt. In his pain he clawed open his shirt
and revealed a raised welt from Max Rosser's
sword-sash circling his neck. Lower down, blood
seeped from his chest. Tibbs's snap shot had hit
the man flush on the breastbone. The slug,
entering at an angle, had slithered along the ribs
and broken out under the armpit.

Turning, Tibbs found Doc Neston behind him, glaring down. His black eyes were slanted under glowering brows. Doc's face was almost black with fury, the thick lips shouting accusations. "What right—what right you got to gun down—"

"Order in this court!" Judge Yontz was bleating. His collar had slipped and was now flapping with each bang of the gavel. He was shocked and exceedingly bitter about the disruption in his court. "I'll have order in this courtroom or—"

"Aw, shut up!" barked Doc Neston. "You're the only one making any racket!"

The remark brought Yontz out of his semihysteria, and he recovered some judicial aplomb. Pointing his gavel at the wounded assassin, he ordered, "Marshal, place that man under arrest!" He whacked the table for the last time and announced, "Court's adjourned!"

"Are you *crazy?*" yelled Doc Neston. "Wes was doing his duty. Rosser was armed. That thieving guerrilla was fixing to escape." He grabbed for Yontz's sleeve. "I'm filing charges against your marshal for shooting down a governor's deputy. If you don't arrest him, my men will!"

With a quizzical look at the judge's shocked face, Orion Tibbs brought his shotgun around and pressed it against Doc Neston's stomach. Despite his fury, Doc sucked in his stomach, his eyes popping.

"Clear the room," the marshal ordered easily. Neston, gritting his jaws, backed off and entered the barroom. Tibbs directed a pair of citizens to lift Wesley Neston. Groaning and waving his arms, Wes was hustled across the street and deposited on a cot in the jail. Tibbs then saw to Max Rosser. This guerrilla, with a price on his head, a killer of fifty-four Yanks and an admitted horse thief, was carried out and deposited in the cold loft of Jeff Glory's barn.

The bounty hunters, regaining their courage with the disappearance of the four-barreled guns, swaggered into the Palace barroom to hold counsel with Doc Neston.

For several hours, waiting for the next move, Pineville lingered on a dead center. The killing of Max Rosser and the arrest of Wesley raised questions that exhausted hours of debate. Was Wesley Neston a murderer, or was he a deputy preventing the prisoner from gunning his way to freedom? Were Marshal Tibbs and Judge Yontz in legal quicksand? By jailing a governor's deputy, had the judge exceeded his authority? Raw emotions sparked the legal complications. Would Doc Neston try to take Tibbs? There was a smacking of expectant lips. An orgy of gunfire had been prevented in the courtroom. The bounty hunters had hung up their gun belts in the anteroom, but now, armed, what would they do?

On the third floor of the Palace, Orion met with Yontz. They stared at the pair of derringers Tibbs had laid on the judge's bed. Against the patchwork quilt they gleamed in the sunlight.

"This one was fired." Orion was making his point, lifting and hefting one stubby gun. "Neston fired one shot. Max Rosser didn't try to draw. When he saw Wesley Neston stand up, Rosser was busy dodging."

"So was I," Yontz admitted with asperity.

"If Rosser had had a gun, he would've fired."

"Then the Nestons killed Rosser in cold blood," boomed Yontz. "When Wesley cut down on the prisoner, one of the others moved up and planted the second gun on Max Rosser. It worked, except that you winged Wesley." A glint of pleasure sparkled in the judge's eyes.

"These two guns match," Tibbs went on.

"And right in my court!" Yontz was again becoming furious. "They set up a murder right under my eyes!"

"Sure they did." Orion was solemn. "We'll

keep young Neston in jail until he's tried for murder."

Judge Yontz shook his head. "Not in my court, Orion." He grew more angry as he faced the complications. "I'm a witness. He'll have to be tried in the Prescott court."

The marshal rose and nodded with a sardonic grimace. "I expect Doc to try to take him out of jail."

"I'm not sure." Yontz was reflective. "There's plenty we don't know about Doc Neston's strategy. Sure, his brother's wounded, but he'll be safe in our jail. You think Doc will blow his chances to take Dixiecity just to have a chance at springing his brother?"

Marshal Tibbs considered this. Certainly Doc Neston had some campaign plan. Nobody, not even the army, would overrun the fortress Captain Murphy had constructed in the Tooloons. And why would Doc be bringing in a crew at the start of winter? Orion shrugged and answered the judge. "Neston's working on something tricky. That's his business. But . . ." Orion paused, thinking hard. As long as those Missouri guerrillas were holed up in Dixiecity and Doc Neston's bounty hunters were around, there would be little peace in this part of the country.

His reflections were interrupted by a loud banging on the door. "Yontz, let me in there!" Doc Neston was shouting and hitting the door panel with a meaty fist.

Yontz walked over and flipped the latch. Doc Neston, holsters filled, stalked in. His size shrank the room. He glared at the derringers before addressing the judge. "You got no right to hold my brother. He's a governor's deputy. He killed a murderer with a bounty on his head."

"Cold-blooded murder." The judge had his dander up. "My orders were no guns permitted. Rosser was unarmed. Your brother shot him, and someone planted that second derringer." He scowled, rising to his full height as he walked forward as though he would stride right through Doc Neston. He halted inches away and glared up into his face. "Was it you?"

Doc wasn't easily cowed but held his temper. "You'll not try Wes for murder?"

Yontz shook his head. "We've already settled that. He's remanded to the marshal. His trial will be held in Prescott."

"But he's wounded," complained Doc with relief.

"He'll be able to travel," Tibbs said. "As soon as Crater Pass opens up, that is."

Doc scowled as he turned back to the door. Invectives were building up, but he only showed his spite by slamming the door.

"What kind of a bluff is he running?" Yontz was half belligerent.

Orion was ironic. "It's his move. But we've got a bag of cougars to drown—or to set free."

"Eh?"

"Wesley Neston killed one of Captain Murphy's men."

"They've been outlawed," Yontz faltered. He sensed Orion's meaning. Outlawed or not, they were mighty mean fighters. "Vengeance is mine" suited their thinking. Maybe, Yontz ruminated, "An eye for an eye" would fit even better. Horseless but with numerical superiority, Captain Murphy's column might try to demolish Pineville, as Quantrill had raided and overrun Lawrence, Kansas.

Tibbs, shrugging Yontz's inane remark aside, put into words what was skipping through the judge's mind. "Doc Neston's got about fourteen men. Captain Murphy's got a full hundred. If Murphy decides to come into Pineville . . ." He allowed the thought to hang there. Just as long as the guerrillas roosted at Dixiecity, Pineville would always be threatened. Manhunters, headquartering at Pineville, would launch their punitive expeditions into the Tooloons.

Another thought nagged at Orion's brain. While in Dixiecity, he had had the thought that Captain Murphy was laying plans to break out. Could Doc Neston have some inside information? Had he guessed Mruphy's intent and was assembling a force to catch the column en route for the border? Also, Dixiecity was living on short rations. Only twelve horses for food and skimpy woodpiles that wouldn't last another two weeks.

"Captain Murphy would be crazy to attack Pineville." Yontz put his own qualms into optimistic words. "Wouldn't he?"

"An attack is sometimes the best defense, Judge," Orion absently answered. "For the peace of this entire area, it would be to our advantage to get Captain Murphy and his guerrillas out of the Tooloons and deep into Mexico. As long as they're holed up in Dixiecity . . ."

7

The early storm continued. Outwardly Pine-ville remained tranquil. Actually, it was like a sparrow seated on an ostrich egg; when hatched, the trouble would be more than the town could handle. Max Rosser's corpse was moved to the old powder shed at Chill Tanks. Wesley Neston claimed bounty on the dead guerrilla, and Yontz decided that the court in Prescott would have to handle that decision, too. The snow from a norther blew in and plastered the town. Crater Pass remained blocked up.

At the jail Wesley Neston grew more irritable as his healing wound itched and tightened. Down at the grove Doc Neston's crew stoked large fires and cussed Tibbs, Yontz, Pineville, and the weather. Enticed north by promises of quick and legal head money, they brooded over the delay. The guerrillas were out of reach as long as the storms piled snow in the Tooloons.

Doc Neston nursed his bruised feelings but was content to allow his brother to occupy Tibbs's jail. Betsy Smith was a capable nurse. The prisoner was being well fed and kept warm. The delay, irksome as it was, actually fitted into Doc Neston's plans to capture or kill a sizable number of Captain Murphy's men.

Marshal Tibbs and Fish-hunter grew weary. As long as Wesley Neston remained in jail, his burly brother was a threat. Tibbs was surprised the showdown hadn't erupted immediately. As the wounded man gained strength, the burning fuse crept closer. One day soon Doc Neston would lead his man hunters up out of the grove and hit the jail.

The close confinement irked Tibbs. He hadn't forgotten Captain Murphy. The news of Rosser's murder would have spread deep into the Tooloons. Someone should be patrolling on the slopes. Sid Peel, overdue from his visit to Piper Garfield, was locked out by the snow clogging Crater Pass. That made it even. Sid was blocked out, but so were Doc Neston's reinforcements. Orion fervently hoped Captain Murphy's column was snowed in so deep that they would have to be dug out.

This uneasy truce, forced on all parties by the inclement weather, did serve to bring Judge Yontz and Orion Tibbs closer to an understanding.

The killing in his court had made a Neston-hater out of the judge. It had also chipped away some of his faith in the new governor. The governor had blandly provided the Neston crew with a hunting license for humans. That act, to Yontz's ethical mind, was sheer hypocrisy. It tainted the governor with the suspicion that he expected to benefit from Neston's manhunt. In addition, Doc Neston's bland assumption that Wesley had a legal right to shoot down Rosser in cold blood was heresy to the circuit judge.

Late in the afternoon of the next day, the judge braved the storm and pounded on the barred door of the marshal's office. "Open up, Marshal," he shouted. "I've got to talk to you."

"Sure, Judge." Tibbs was standing behind his visitor.

Startled, the judge swung around. Tibbs, the four-barreled gun cradled in his elbow, had been standing guard at one corner of the fieldstone building. "That blasted thing!" Being startled made the judge sarcastic. "You sleep with it?"

"And it also shares my meals," Tibbs calmly replied. He pushed past the judge and rapped twice on the door. "Let's get out of the snow." Fishhunter swung the heavy door open for their entrance.

Standing in front of the small stove, Sid Peel

was blowing across the top of his coffee cup. The banty-sized deputy tipped his tin cup in a sardonic salute to Yontz.

The judge, caught off balance, stared. A storm-damp sheepskin coat was draped over the back of a stool. Sid's chaps, plain batwings that hung over his instep, were stained by water. Behind his straggling whiskers, Sid's face was pinched inward by fatigue.

Open-mouthed, Yontz demanded, "Is the Pass open? And how'd you get in without anyone knowing?"

Sid took another sip of coffee, shook his head, and maintained his owlish stare.

Orion laughed. "The judge is still on our side, Sid. Tell him."

"Tell me what?" the judge began caustically. "And what do you mean"—he turned on Orion—"I'm *still* on your side?"

Sid took the floor. "I walked in, mostly." He sounded important and began a bandy-legged pacing. "Crater Pass is a mess. Blocked from both sides. Wagons and buckboards is all stuck, hub-deep." He halted to grin and ask, "Who do you suppose is hung up right on top?"

"Jeff Glory, of course," replied Yontz with satisfaction. "He was in such a hurry to claim bounty, he'd have tried to tunnel through an iceberg."

"Don't fret about Jeff," Sid said. "Anybody tries to take those two bodies will get all eight slugs from a Henry rifle."

"Never mind about Jeff Glory," Yontz prodded. "How come you're here *if* that Pass is plugged?"

Sid Peel explained briefly. He had backed off the Pass, circled around through the canyon along the Apache Trail, then crossed Cold Ravine via Grass Lake.

"Nobody ever walked across Grass Lake!" the judge scoffed.

"You asked, and I'm telling you," declared Sid Peel.

"It's frozen over," Tibbs explained to the bewildered judge. "Sid and his horse walked it." There was pride in the marshal's voice. Sid straightened his bony shoulders and nodded.

"And that explains that," the judge said, dismissing the subject. "You talk to Piper Garfield? Were his cattle stolen?"

"First things first, Judge," Tibbs cut in. "Let Sid finish." He reached out an arm to halt Sid's jaunty pacing and urged, "Tell the judge about Bend Bow Canyon."

"Cleaned by the hard wind. Hardly no snow a'tall. It was the easiest part of the trip. I crossed that ridge about half a mile from Dixiecity. Easy walking."

"You telling me that Crater Pass is plugged and you've hiked across the Tooloons?" demanded the judge.

"A freak of nature," admitted Tibbs. "Now, let's make it work for us."

"You can't take Wesley Neston out that way!" Yontz, misunderstanding, objected with dismay. "In this weather he can't walk that far. Besides—"

"We know that," the marshal interrupted, frowning. "But getting that gun-happy kid out of Pineville is the least of our problems. Listen, if Sid can walk in, can't Captain Murphy's guerrillas walk out? Our worry is, which way will they walk?"

"You still believe Captain Murphy might move in on Pineville?"

Marshal Tibbs nodded. "Don't forget Max Rosser. Captain Murphy sets a mighty lot of store on every man he's got. To have a soldier murdered in a law court . . ." Tibbs left the ominous sentence hanging.

Judge Yontz flinched and asked, "What do you suggest?"

Tibbs again proceeded to reason out the problems that confronted Pineville. Doc Neston had established a man-hunters' camp late in the fall. It would take time to bring in sufficient men to attempt an assault on Dixiecity. Such an assault, in Orion's belief, was doomed to failure. Captain Murphy had already fought off one army. He was well fortified and with deadly mountain howitzers in his possession. Short of food, he obviously intended to eat those spavined animals harbored in his headquarters. But twelve horses wouldn't feed a hundred men until spring. Therefore, he intended to escape.

Doc Neston had to be aware of Captain Murphy's dilemma. Neston expected to catch the guerrillas out in the open and cut the column to pieces.

"You mean walk out during the winter?" Yontz was having difficulty believing that men would take such a gamble. "Captain Murphy expects to outwalk the mounted man hunters?" He shook his head in dismay. "Clear to the Mexican border?"

"Or into Pineville," Orion quietly added.

"Lord on high!" Yontz exploded. "Doc Neston knows, and knew it all along, that Murphy's going to come out? But he figures the retreat will be to the border? Captain Murphy may be waiting until Neston gathers his full force. Then he could move on Pineville, knock out Neston's crew, take his animals, and head south!"

Orion poured himself a cup of coffee and let the worried judge speculate. In his summing up, the judge had missed one ingredient—revenge. The acquisition of horses and supplies was, until Max Rosser's murder, a prime reason for attacking Pineville. Now Captain Murphy would want much more. Wesley Neston would be the prime target, followed by Doc Neston. Then Judge Yontz, who had supported the governor's program and allowed Rosser to be killed without a trial, would be next. And the Pineville marshal? Orion winced. He, too, had let Max Rosser down.

"That's just what I'd do myself!" Yontz boomed out so loud that even Sid Peel jumped. Yontz's cherubic face was a mass of wrinkles, and he was thinking of it while he talked. "There's one flaw in that kind of raid," he began. "Say the raid was successful; they got the horses and whipped the Neston gang. So. Tell me, Marshal, how'd Captain Murphy get his men over the Pass? They'd never have a chance to reach the border. They'd be bottled up right here until the governor could send in soldiers."

"That stumped me, too, until Sid walked in," admitted the marshal.

"But Murphy can't know about that route." Yontz's statement was regretful. He reflected on Tibbs's statement and demanded with a hint of anger, "It sounds as if you *want* that guerrilla column to escape to Mexico!"

"That'd make it better for everyone," Orion blandly admitted. "You know any other marshal who wants a hundred legal outlaws camping in his jurisdiction?"

"Legal outlaws! Why, they're—"

"The governor refused them amnesty. That makes them men without a country. They're not subject to laws, are they? And they have a right to survive. To fight for their lives." Orion watched Yontz's mouth fall open and quickly changed the subject. "But we've only told you the bad part."

"There's more? Something that makes sense?"

Orion nodded to hide a smile and addressed Sid Peel. "Tell the Judge about Piper Garfield."

Sid, locking his hands behind his back, resumed his pacing. "Piper's from Cass County, Missouri. The Garfields go way back. When the Federal General Order Number Eleven was issued, some of the Garfield kin was plundered. He ain't a bit mad at them Rebels in Dixiecity."

Judge Yontz again exploded. "But Piper's been complaining for months about losing cattle and horses in the Tooloons! Isn't that why the marshal sent you down there to see him?"

"If you want to believe it," grunted Sid Peel, and grew silent.

"Well, go on, Sid," Yontz avidly urged. "So Piper isn't mad at the guerrillas. What does that mean?"

Orion took over. "It means we can sneak Captain Murphy's men out the back way, just like Sid came in. Once on the far side of the mountains, we can get Piper to loan them horses."

"A hundred horses?" Yontz knew he sounded foolish, but each of them—Tibbs, Sid Peel, and even the silent Fish-hunter—was confusing everything. First there was talk of a raid on Pineville, a war right at home with Murphy's guerrillas and Doc Neston's gang fighting it out. It was enough to scare a man half to death, such talk. Then Tibbs was calmly pointing out that they could walk the guerrilla column out of the Tooloons and arrange for Garfield horses to carry them across the Mexican border. Completely illegal, and asking a federal judge to be a party to the scheme!

"Piper's got a thousand horses." Fish-hunter's suave words shattered Yontz's churning thoughts.

"Does it all have to be decided right now? This afternoon?" Yontz asked plaintively. Actually, it did seem a proper solution. Pineville would be spared. Hadn't there been enough blood spilled in the streets? But the governor? Yontz's judgment faltered. This wild plan had been broached too suddenly. "Please," Yonz begged, "can't we think about it?"

"You do that, Judge." Tibbs was cryptic. "You think about it."

"What will you do, Marshal?"

"Just sit here and worry." Orion lifted the coffeepot and was pouring as Judge Oleander Yontz tottered out.

8

Judge Yontz awakened to the thunder of cannon. He lay still, waiting for his tired mind to clear. In the gloom he could see the stack of lawbooks on the desk. A bottle of whiskey was balanced on the edge of a straight chair. He had spent the night with lawbooks and the bottle. There were so very many contradictions. The jumbled case should be called "A Marshal's Authority versus the Governor's Orders." Tibbs had shot down Wesley Neston and jailed the man who, supposedly, had a legal right to kill Max Rosser. The governor would take a dim view of Tibbs's act. There was the added threat that Doc Neston would overrun the jail and gun down Tibbs. And to top off the pure lunacy of it all, Tibbs wanted to aid the guerrilla column's escape.

Yontz had drawn a blank with the lawbooks, but whiskey had allowed his tired brain to relax. He had drifted off finally and roused to the thump of cannon fire. What the glory was going on?

Yontz hurried to the window. The snow had stopped. Dawn was filtering through heavy clouds. While he watched, an exploding shell hit the marshal's office. The thick door was blown inward and smoke began to drift out.

Numbed, his stomach a hollow, the judge stared as another shell smashed against the jail wall. Chunks of adobe rose with the black smoke. Yontz groaned; the cells were on that side.

Another flash of fire brought him around. In the cottonwood grave a wagon, its canvas afire, had been overturned. He could hear shouts and the squeal of horses. Outlined by the flames, men dodged among the tree trunks. There had to be two gun crews to account for the lines of fire.

The first barrage had shattered the marshal's office, and shells were now battering Main Street. He felt the Palace take a round as the frame building shook, and he heard the crash of glass. The smell of black powder seeped upward. Yontz raised the window. Cold air cut through his shirt. Jeff Glory's stable was afire. The bombardment blended with the screams of trapped horses.

Tactics, Yontz knew, would send skirmishers to race in under the cover fire. He reached for his smooth bore, laid the barrel on the damp sill, and waited for a target. The howitzer fire tracked back up the street. The Palace took another shock, somewhere on the lower floor, which jolted the fieldrock foundations.

The cannonade died. There was no rush of screaming Rebels. The fire at the marshal's office crackled. Men shouted as they fought to save fire-crazed horses. In the grove the wagon still burned. Flames had leaped into the lower tree branches and were smothered by clinging snow. On the cold morning air a single Rebel yell drifted up from the buffalo ponds.

The attack was over. Yontz leaned back, crammed the tail of his nightshirt back into his drawers, and smiled thinly. He had the decision that had escaped him the night before. Marshal Tibbs had to be gotten out of Pineville! Let him lead Captain Murphy's column out. That would take days.

Once Crater Pass opened, it was a circuit judge's duty to carry that information to Prescott. The Federal army could intervene and block the escape. Without horses on the flatlands, the guerrillas would be quickly rounded up. And Tibbs? Well, he would have to fend for himself. Yontz recognized that he was on shaky legal ground and a Judas to inflict harm upon the dedicated marshal; however, it was a practical solution. The threat from the guerrillas would end. Doc Neston's killers would be out of Pineville, and this crazy war would be over.

Knowing he was rationalizing in circles, Yontz began to dress. Had Captain Murphy simply vented his wrath on Pineville? What next? Yontz flicked a hurried glance at the jail. The bars on Wesley Neston's cell were torn apart. Yontz whistled. What if Wesley Neston were dead? As soon as they recovered, Neston would lead his gang against Tibbs. Armed with those violent four-barreled weapons, the Pineville law officers would fight to the death.

Yontz hurried into the street. The shell that had fired Jeff Glory's barn had torn out an entire wall. Through the splintered studs men were herding animals into the alleyway. On the hotel porch Betsy Smith swatted at a small blaze with a smoldering broom. Belligerently she turned on the judge.

"What under the sun happened?" she asked.

"The civil war finally reached Arizona," he quipped, and crossed the street.

Looking into the jail, he saw smoke still puffing from the cell block. Behind him awed citizens were gathering as he entered. The room smelled of explosives. The stove had tipped, and hot coals rolled across the floor. Beyond, in the back cells, more smoke gathered.

Sid Peel was crumpled behind the overturned desk. "Wanted" posters had blown over his frame. When Yontz lifted him, Sid groaned. Dragging the deputy into the street, Yontz turned as Marshal Tibbs staggered out.

Tibbs clung to the riot gun. His eyes were dulled from shock. A trickle of blood dripped from a gash on his cheek bone.

"What about Wesley Neston?" Yontz asked with fleeting hope.

Orion's head was clearing in the crisp air, but his voice was thick as he shook his head. "Direct hit on his cell. Neston's dead."

"You think it's over?" The judge looked around anxiously.

"Only in town." Tibbs pointed to the Neston camp. A rattle of rifle shots, spaced by Colt fire, was still going on. Down in the grove Murphy's men were still seeking live targets.

"Round up some men," Orion ordered. "Bring them down to the grove." He bent over Sid Peel; then, relieved, he added, "Have someone get Sid over to the hotel. Betsy will know what to do."

Yontz nodded and raised Sid to his feet. When he looked up, the marshal was trotting toward the cottonwood grove. Yontz stared at his own hands. They were trembling. Self-incrimination flowed over him. Why hadn't he acted yesterday? Agreed to allow Tibbs to help Captain Murphy's men to escape? Would his agreement have prevented this attack? Yontz doubted it, but, shaking himself to control a shiver, he decided in the future that he would listen more closely to Tibbs's suggestions.

Marshal Tibbs approached the grove with caution. The gunfire had turned sporadic. The grove had been well defended. Cannon fire hadn't knocked out Doc Neston's crew. Veterans of infighting, they clung to the protection of the tree trunks and sniped at powder flashes. Orion, guessing the guerrillas' strategy, turned toward the Nestons' horse pen. A crazy thought flashed through his mind. Would Murphy's men choose fat ones for eating or—?

Keening Rebel yelps, more like screeches of jubilation, rose above the sounds of battle. Orion raised himself to look. A man was trying to mount a bucking horse. It was the long-haired sentry he had overpowered at the Dixiecity guardhouse. He was aboard now, and the lunging horse broke past Orion, who came sharply about, gun raised, but they were out of shotgun range.

Quiet settled over the grove. Doc Neston's camp was in ruins. Wagon gear smelling of burned oiled leather permeated the camp. Tree branches dropped sparks on burned canvas and woolen blankets. One howitzer shell had felled a huge tree onto the sleeping area, and several men were poking through the mess.

Doc Neston stomped up from the horse pen. His face was soot-blackened. He cradled a rifle, stuffing shells into the side breech. "Wasn't no more'n ten of 'em," he growled as he halted in front of Tibbs. "Only got away with one horse." He sounded puzzled.

Orion understood. Why had the attackers simply faded away? He could picture them tramping through the fresh snow and returning to the safety of the Tooloons. Had the attack on the grove been a diversion, a ploy, so they could smash the jail and kill Wesley Neston?

"Anyone hurt?" Tibbs asked.

"Some wounded, nobody killed," was the terse reply. "Scattered our gear. That's about the worst."

Slowly, Tibbs started to shake his head, locking Doc's angry eyes with his own. "The worst was at the jail." Dismay flooded the burly face before him.

"The kid?"

"They hit it twice. Wounded my deputy and killed your brother."

Doc Neston's firm hand slipped in the next shell. He reached to extract another cartridge from his belt. The leather cuff held the wrist firm, but his fingers were shaking. He looked into Tibbs's eyes and coolly asked, "An eye for an eye?"

Orion half nodded. "He threw his weight at the jail. Kept everyone pinned down. Making you figure he'd come for your horses."

Doc Neston's face contorted and he snarled, "That's the last prisoner you'll lose!"

Expecting Neston to level the rifle and fire, Orion batted the barrel with his free hand. He brought the four barrels up even with Neston's stomach at the same moment.

Doc Neston turned slowly, then, with head bowed and lips moving, walked away. Orion couldn't tell whether the bounty hunter was praying or cursing.

Suddenly a horse screamed in pain and we heard Doc Neston shout, "Somebody shoot that critter! We all gotta die sometime!"

Orion Tibbs, followed by Judge Yontz, entered Sid Peel's room. He had been patched up by Betsy Smith. She had wound a bandage turban that was almost large enough to overbalance his rakish head. Sid wore a self-conscious smirk.

"Seems to me, Judge," Orion sadly began, "we've worn out a lawman."

"That's right," agreed the judge. "Not much

staying power. When they're needed, they're laid up somewhere or other."

Sid's eyes widened and he instantly fought back. "You ever tried fightin' off Betsy when she's ordered to nurse someone?"

"Ordered?" Yontz was shocked. "Who ordered what?"

"You did and you know it!" Sid was growling now. "You told Betsy she was to patch me up." He clawed at the bandage. "An' look what she done!" He flung back the blanket and sat up. Dizzy for a second, he braced his arms on the mattress, his muscles like braided cords of rawhide.

Orion looked at Yontz and they both shook their heads.

"Now, none of that!" Sid pulled himself together and shouted. "You come up here for a reason. It wasn't just to look in on a wounded old buck now, was it?"

Orion smiled warmly toward Yontz and stated, "Like I said, Judge, we can depend on Sid. All my deputies are wang leather and loop tight."

"You only got *two*," retorted Sid. "Doc Neston coming gunning? I guessed he would with Wesley dead and all. He figures we're to blame 'cause we're closest, eh?"

Orion grew serious. "We've got to get Captain Murphy and his men down into Mexico."

Judge Yontz noted the suspicion in Sid Peel's eyes and said hurriedly, "It's the only way. As long as they're squatting up there at Dixiecity with their stingers ready, we'll have fighting. A dang feud going on with Doc Neston's men and—"

Orion broke in, "Sid, you're going on ahead. Same way you came in. You're to locate Piper Garfield and arrange for that horse relay."

"Fine. Can do." Sid began to pull on a boot. He looked up to ask, "Fish-hunter? He going?"

"He's gone already," Tibbs told him. "He's two hours out, heading for Mexico."

"What for?" Sid demanded. "To locate a hideaway for us? When the governor finds out we helped them Rebs escape, we'll need it."

"No cause to worry." Judge Yontz covered his own confusion with judicial pomposity. "The function of the law is to protect as well as to punish. The lives and welfare of every man, woman, and child in the territory could become involved." Logically, Yontz knew Tibbs's plan was proper. By removing the source of the irritation, the disease could be cured. But the governor would have to be the final judge. Yontz excused his own trickery by self-righteous moralizing. Perhaps Tibbs could get the guerrillas out of the Tooloons and save this district from becoming involved in a mass killing. It was only right that the Federal soldiers could round them up out on the flatlands.

"Fish-hunter is to locate Colonel Grey's brigade." Orion was filling in the deputy. "Captain Murphy may need some help getting across the border. Fish-hunter will have to locate the brigade and bring them back to Sasabe." He waited for Sid's nod of understanding, then solemnly added, "Now I'm afraid I have to tell you some bad news."

"And what's that?" Sid's eyes bugged.

"You'll have to take off those boots to get your pants on."

9

Halfway up the mountain, on the Dixiecity trail, Mick's ears flickered nervously. Orion snubbed the lead rope of the pack train and patted Mick's neck. "Right about here, Mick, did someone hit you with a rock?" Mick bobbed his head as though in affirmation until the bridle jingled.

This had been Max Rosser's ambush. His carbine slugs had skipped through these manzanitas. It had been snowing then, but now clouds scudded overhead and sent waves of shadows along the mountainside. That early storm and Max Rosser were both dead.

This had nagged Tibbs since he left Pineville. He had forced Captain Murphy to surrender the soldier. When Rosser was gunned down in Yontz's courtroom, Murphy had brought his guns off the mountain and avenged the soldier's killing. Would Captain Murphy ever trust a lawman again?

Trusting Tibbs was the guerrillas' only hope.

With Crater Pass blocked, the beleagured Rebels were like a ship locked in an iceflow until Sid Peel discovered the open channel. With Grass Lake frozen, Murphy could walk his men through Cold Ravine. The Apache trail would take them down the mountain. The provisions carried by Orion's pack train would last until they could break into the desert flatlands. Then, mounted by Piper Garfield's fresh horses, they could race for the Mexican border. That was where the real danger existed, from the Federal cavalry stationed along the border. Given time and some luck, Fishhunter could take care of that.

Orion grimaced. If it were only that simple. The skeptical guerrilla officer had to be convinced that a local marshal, with the unwilling support of a Federal judge, was willing to aid the escape of a company of posted Rebels. Might not he think the hidden exit trail a trap? Or a trick to entice the defenders out of their fortress so that Doc Neston could pick them off?

Orion blocked these thoughts from his mind. Captain Murphy would simply have to understand that it was the only way out, he decided, and led his pack train onto the last rocky ridge.

The ice had disappeared. Water seeped from beneath the packed snowpack. Below, in the dark canyons, the chill would be worse. The ice already formed would last out the winter. Crater Pass, exposed to the wind, would open up.

This thought worried Orion. Doc Neston would be nosing around to discover where all three Pineville lawmen had gone. Judge Yontz had a ready story about an Apache raiding party sighted near Mountain Meadows. Wasn't it natural that the Pineville officers would go out and investigate? Ben Bolt had helped load the pack animals by lantern light and promised to hold his tongue. At the time it hadn't worried Tibbs. Doc Neston was undermanned. But if Crater Pass opened up, the bounty hunters would pour in like scavengers. Doc Neston had been patient, and Orion guessed that he had information about Captain Murphy's attempting a winter breakout. Like a pack of wolves, the man hunters intended to pick the guerrillas off like hamstrung buffalo.

A carbine cracked twice and drove further thoughts from Orion Tibbs's mind. Mick shied. Orion reined in, clasped his hands on the pommel, and waited.

Captain Murphy, angry eyes locked on Orion's face, whirled about. The pacing bootheels advanced across the uneven floor. Orion noted that the horses had been moved to the outside corral to mingle with two animals brought back from the raid on Doc Neston's camp. Ushered across the parade ground, he had observed that the guerrillas were mustered to march. Packs, pitifully small, were arranged along the barrack walls.

"You bear a charmed life," Captain Murphy rasped. "Why didn't they shoot you?" He clucked with reluctant admiration, "Riding in here cold, with our picket lines alerted for a possible attack."

"I was in a hurry to get here before you moved out," Orion answered.

Captain Murphy was grim. "And how did you —or anyone else—know we were moving out?"

"Small woodpiles," Orion replied laconically.

Halting, the officer gasped, "What?"

"If you had intended to winter in," Orion explained, "you'd have firewood tiered all over this place."

"So you figured cavalry could walk?"

Orion shrugged. "Cavalry are mounted infantry."

"Just short woodpiles?" The captain looked thoughtful. "That all you figured it on?"

"There's more, Captain. Twelve horses won't feed a hundred men through the winter. But they could get you out of the mountains."

"And who else is aware that we plan to march

out?" Captain Murphy kept the deep concern out of the question, but his face had hardened.

"You've had deserters?"

"Four. They left about six weeks back," Murphy admitted. He relaxed a bit. The sparring was finished. Orion felt that mutual trust had been established.

Orion Tibbs expressed his concern. Somehow Doc Neston had learned that the guerrillas would attempt a breakout. The bounty hunter had moved into Pineville in the late fall. He had set up camp and his man hunters were gathering. A direct winter attack on Dixiecity, or a siege, was futile. Heavy snows would prevent such a direct attack. These same snows would contain the defenders. So, as far as Doc Neston was concerned, even the exact timing wasn't too important. The border was a long way off. Afoot, without the protection of these stout walls, Murphy's men could be rounded up like Texas beef.

Captain Murphy allowed Orion to finish, then smiled thinly. "It's been planned. We've rationed food. And that's why the short woodpiles. Once Garfield moved his herd off summer pasture, it's been slim pickings."

"Then now is the time to get out," Orion stated.

"With Crater Pass blocked?" Murphy's voice was hollow. "We've smashed Neston's camp and have two of his fresh horses to carry our howitzers, but how do we get out? We know a large number of Neston's recruits are waiting to come in over the Pass. Afoot, we'd be overrun and cornered in the Pass."

"There's a second route." The captain's head came up as Orion elaborated. He told of Sid Peel's detour across Grass Lake and up Cold Ravine. The officer began his pacing again.

"Even the deserters, or whoever Neston's receiving his information from, wouldn't know about that route." Captain Murphy reached his decision. "I'll brief my staff."

Captain Murphy's staff consisted of two lieutenants and a pair of sergeants. All were lithe as buggy whips. Orion had the impression they were ready to lash out, scar the hide, and draw blood. They gathered quickly, the officers seated around the table and the deferential noncoms standing.

The briefing was swift. Murphy passed on the information Orion had brought in. Four pairs of inquisitive eyes studied the marshal. Suspicion, heavy enough to taste, scented the large room.

"This information may be correct," probed a lieutenant, "but can we trust the Yank?"

"Leave the sarcasm for the ranks, Lieutenant

Hinds!" snapped Captain Murphy. "*I* believe the Marshal. His motives are logical. We may mistrust his sympathies, but we can control his behavior. Sergeant Rosser, step forward, please."

Orion Tibbs could understand the captain's attitude. The man was a trained soldier. He could submerge his likes and dislikes to save his men. And his ace in the hole was this grizzled sergeant.

"Marshal, Sergeant Rosser is Max Rosser's father. I commit you to his charge. It will be left in his judgment to prevent you from jeopardizing our chances to reach the Mexican border. Understand?" He paused. "Anything else, Marshal?"

Orion studied the sergeant. A razorback of a man in his late forties. The stubble on his lean face was white and needle-sharp. Wrinkles worked from his forehead and gathered his ageless eyes into a squint. This man could kill and bunk down next to the corpse. He had lived with death and learned to ignore it. Sergeant Rosser would need no motive to kill a marshal—only orders. The grizzled fighter would support Doc Neston's creed: "Everybody has to die."

Tibbs was as terse as the officer. "Don't delay, Captain. You're packed; move out. A hundred men will leave a fair-sized track. There's another storm due. It can cover our tracks. Above all, don't underrate Doc Neston. He just might have a scout or two back in the brush." He smiled grimly. "Let me have Sergeant Rosser and we'll lead out. Give us a half hour, then pick up our trail. If we can get down off these ridges before dark, our trail should be blotted out before morning."

"Correct, Marshal Tibbs. We'll move out at once." Captain Murphy turned back to his staff. There was steel in his quiet orders. "Handguns and howitzers. Divide up the canister and solid shot. Every man is to carry, in addition to his handguns, a full hudred rounds of ammunition. Lieutenant Hinds, you'll remain here for two full hours. You will then fire the fort and support us as rear guard."

"Fire the fort?" Lieutenant Hinds repeated numbly.

"We won't be coming back." Captain Murphy's voice was firm.

10

Pineville was explosive the evening that Marshal Tibbs had led his pack train toward Dixiecity. The bounty hunters' camp in the grove had survived Captain Murphy's cannonade. It was a tight-lipped Doc who arranged Wesley Neston's burial. Max Rosser's killing in Judge Yontz's courtroom, and the subsequent howitzer attack, had sobered the local citizens. They stayed off the streets. The last twenty-four hours had introduced insurrection to Pineville, and the sample had been bitter.

The Texas man hunters had unplugged Carter Pass. Hungry for bounty, they had corduroyed an opening across the snowpack. Using tamarack, mesquite, and stunted pines, they heaved, wrestled, and lashed their horses along the narrow roadway. Once free of the snow-glutted cut, they surged hell-for-leather into town.

Gathered in Carlos's Cantina and the Palace Hotel bar, they were indeed a crusty lot. A preacher would have sworn they were escapees from Hades. A doctor would have clucked in amazement at the scars left by cuts and hot lead. Carlos and Barnaby Able nodded in appreciation at their capacity for raw spirits. Judge Yontz searched his memory to connect them with those who had paraded in his court.

One greasy man in a buffalo cape spoke with a true Bostonian accent. A dandy, festooned with silver rosettes on a white lambskin jacket and a tinkling set of spike spurs, spoke only border Spanish. His mean eyes and abrupt gestures conveyed his meaning. All the hunters wore their holsters tied down and carried short-barreled rifles in saddle scabbards. Stiff-backed, tight-lipped, with the glinting seven-pointed stars pinned on their chests, they clinked their 'dobe dollars on the bars and waited for Doc Neston.

He came up from the cemetery like a bull ready to trample a nest of snakes. Yontz, seated in the Palace with Ben Bolt, caught Doc Neston's full fury.

"Where's that blamed Marshal?" Neston asked evenly.

"They're all out scouting Apaches," lied Yontz. "Tibbs and both deputies." It was so raw, Ben Bold shifted uneasily.

"You're telling me," Neston smirked, "with your lying tongue hanging out, that all three of your so-called lawmen've gone out Apache scouting? And all the time you got the look of an egg-stealing hound!"

"It is unusual," Yontz admitted lamely.

"Your town was half blowed apart by them Rebel cannon!" Neston charged, moving forward until his huge shadow fell across the men. "And your law officers figure it's safer trailing Apaches, 'cause they just ain't no Apaches this far north?"

Judge Yontz was grateful that Neston believed Tibbs had left town to avoid trouble. He ducked his head and remained silent.

Doc Neston turned to Ben Bolt. "Mr. Storekeeper, you'd better get along," he ordered. "We'll be needing plenty of chow. Once they soak up their likker, these Tex-a-helligans are gonna be as hungry as seven hundred dollars."

Barnaby Able flipped a bar towel and poked his head over the batwings to announce, "Judge, there's one more coming in. From here it looks like that Fred Wade."

With weary resignation Yontz rose to stare out. Then he sagged back into his seat. Pineville was getting more than a fair share of hard cases. Fred Wade was the governor's number-one hatchet man. He wore Badge Number One. It was a license. Without it he would have been hung for several murders. Yontz had one comforting thought: Marshal Tibbs was out of town. Wade still carried Tibbs's slug in the hip, and he had vowed to cut Tibbs down on the next go-round.

Yontz glanced back. Doc Neston, unblinking, was facing Ben Bolt. Bolt's face was white, and he had slumped like a man with an uneasy stomach. Now he started to rise.

"Hold it right there, storekeeper." Ben Bolt looked as if he had just bitten his tongue as Doc bent to leer into his face. "You got plenty of beans and flour? Maybe some lean bacon? Our cook's got fifty posse to feed."

Relief flooded Ben Bolt's face. His voice was strong as he answered, "Beans and flour and some canned tomatoes, but Marshal Tibbs took all the bacon." He clapped a hand to his mouth as his eyes showed his alarm.

"So. You've joined the club?" Doc Neston, pleased as a sleepy grizzly, hooked a fist into Ben Bolt's suspenders and tugged. "Just where did our marshal take all that bacon?"

Ben made an effort. "The judge told you! Tibbs is chasing Apaches." He ducked his head as though he expected to be hit.

During the moment of silence, bootheels marched across the porch and Fred Wade entered the dim room. A box-like man, he wore a Zuni vest with a serpent and an eagle tattooed on the leather; three rattlesnake buttons dangled from his snakeskin hatband. His gun belt was the cream of Mexican leather work. The braided holsters were tied down around his stocky thighs. He wore his leather pants outside his boots, but the toes were needlepoints protected by silver.

Nodding briefly to Doc Neston, Wade advanced. Doc loosed his hold on Ben Bolt and, with an appreciative glint, nodded for Wade to take over.

"Just where did you say the marshal is chasing these Apaches?" Wade demanded.

Ben Bolt was awed into stunned silence. His mouth worked soundlessly. He watched Wade tip back his hat and heard the snake buttons rattle.

Fred Wade gave him a jab with a thumb and explained, "Mr. Bolt, the governor's bounty includes anyone aiding these Rebels—savvy? The governor would be upset if he believed a Pineville merchant was furnishing supplies to our enemies."

Juge Yontz rose to his feet and glared into the tormentor's face. "Ben sells supplies. It was me and Tibbs who bought the bacon." His voice rose in anger. "And the beans! And the flour!" In the sudden silence, he added, "And what we did with them is our own business!"

Wade sneered. "Your business is upholding the law!"

"As *I* see it, yes." Yontz returned the sneer. "Why were you sent in? To tally the dead?"

Doc Neston cut off the discussion. "Storeman, get on back to your store. We'll do without the bacon." He turned a stalker's face to Wade. "They've cut out of Dixiecity." He laughed as he added, "They're afoot. It'll be like shooting ducks in a bird cage. Them we don't get on the Pass, we'll gun down on the flat!" Doc Neston turned and stomped for the door.

With a leer in the judge's direction, Fred Wade followed.

Captain Murphy's column entered Cold Ravine after dark. Tibbs and Sergeant Rosser watched them come in. Pack straps bit into their narrow shoulders. The packs, a rolled blanket fettered with ties at each end, were woefully thin. A few men carried canteens. Some held a cooking pot or a battered frying pan. Yet the spirit was there. Orion recalled a picture of a drummer, a flag, and a fife. But these men had been denied the flag, and so were exiles in their homeland.

Brush lined the steep walls. Iced-over willows and wild blackberry made progress slow. Men floundered to a halt, located sticks in the underbrush, and lighted small fires. In the flickering, smoking flames, their faces were gaunt.

Sergeant Rosser dangled bacon on a sharpened ramrod and caught the dripping fat in a bare hand. He licked his fingers and softly muttered, "Sure enough beats hoss meat."

Orion nodded. Rosser had been practically mute since leaving Dixiecity. The man's eye sockets were so deep, Orion felt he was looking into a skull. And those sunken eyes had been studying him.

"I been meaning to ask you, Marshal"—the man sounded drained—"about my boy, Max." He lifted the ramrod and slipped the dripping bacon onto his lap. "Max was the last of my four boys. He had plenty of knots in that silk sash of his. That's about all he lived for—to kill Yanks." Rosser's voice firmed. "Did you bury him, sash and all?" He sank his yellowed teeth into the bacon and went on, "I sure would've liked to've had that sash."

Captain Murphy was crossing the ravine. Sergeant Rosser gathered his pack and moved a few yards away. Murphy stopped and studied Tibbs with quizzical eyes. "Still expect that storm, Tibbs?"

"It's coming in, right on time."

The captain waved an arm. "An iceberg in a desert. Nothing like this in Missouri. When will we get below the snowline?"

"Can your men march tonight?"

"If it's necessary."

"Anyone gives out, hoist him onto a horse. I'll take the sergeant and break trail." Orion pointed south. "Thirty miles below here we join the Apache trail. It's protected by an overhang, and there's an Indian hunting camp. Some old hogans and plenty of water. When we get there, we'll be below the snowline and be able to rest."

The captain leaned over the fire, savoring the smell of the bacon. "Thirty miles? Every man's carrying a fifty-pound pack."

"Why fifty pounds?" Orion asked.

Captain Murphy was both evasive and cryptic. "Firepower, Marshal. Guerrillas, firepower."

"Sure, sure." Orion dropped the subject. "We'll move before the men stiffen up."

11

The Arizona Territory was awakening to learn
that it had a political bullwhip cracking around
its ears. News of the governor's bounty hunters
converging on Pineville opened old wounds and
festered prejudices. Humbled Southern soldiers
had sought passive sanctuary in the mountains
and on the sandy plains along the border. These
men understood Captain Murphy's entrapment.
The guerrillas were villains because they had
fought on the losing side. Quantrill, Gater Grey,
and Mosby, branded by the North with the mark
of Cain, were outlawed. Now this new governor at
Prescott was bringing in Texas guns to hunt the
beleaguered Missourians to the death.

Other Arizona citizens, grieved by the importa-
tion of Texas bounty men, wondered why that
money shouldn't be paid out to the natives. Some
resented the governor's interference with local
legal practices. Didn't Pineville and the Tooloons
have a judge? And a real marshal? Many remembered Tibbs's previous excursions south. He had

traveled into Mexico on the trail of Gobal's ban-
ditti; had fought a battle at Barrel Wells against
raiders from south of the border. If that fool governor had any sense, he would have allowed Yontz
and Tibbs to play out their own game with Captain Murphy's column.

Piper Garfield, the territory's cattle baron,
finishing up a drunk in Yuma, sagely remarked,
"That country up there is a snakepit, 'ceptin' the
snakes don't grow rattles. They're mean, but they
don't advertise. Understand?" He thought about
that and tried to clear it up. "Them two, Judge
Yontz and Tibbs, savvy? They go all out. Anybody gets caught in between gets smashed." He
studied his glass while a huge tear rolled down his
weathered cheek. "Think of the pity of it all. Doc
Neston's boys, brave Texas whistlers, and Captain
Murphy's column, which fought until they was
drove back into the Tooloons." A second tear
rolled down the other cheek and he blubbered,
"Both them crews set against the other. Nobody'll
know who's runnin' and who's cashin'." He
finished his drink and marched out of the saloon
with a wishful thought. "One thing's for sure. I'd
like a ticket for the finish."

Judge Yontz, en route to Prescott, was seated
behind a light team dodging the muck thrown up

by the straining horses. He was entering Crater Pass and wondering if he could get the buckboard through. The Pass, an inverted saucer huddling under a tower of cracked lava, was formidable at any time of the year. And now it filled with snow, and the lava ridge was a mass of ice. The corduroy road had sunk as the snowbanks sagged inward.

He glanced toward Dixiecity. Ridge after ridge, all clothed in forest, were like a giant's washboard. The canyons were so deep and so dark that men felt smothered. Grass Lake, a wide stretch of swamp edged by sword grass, was an animal's burial ground. Yontz clucked to himself. If Orion Tibbs could lead a hundred men through these mountains, one Judge Yontz should be able to force a buckboard over Crater Pass.

"Ha-lle-ooo!" The spectral call brought Yontz around. A man was floundering forward, a hat tied over his head with a red bandanna. Whiskers covered fat cheeks, and his entire body shook with ague. The tip of a pegleg was wrapped in sacking. Yontz reined in. The horses blew and, trembling, pulled away from the approaching creature.

"It's Jeff Glory!" the man shouted. "That you, Judge?"

"You're spooking the horses!" Yontz snapped.

"Shouldn't wonder. They're afraid I'll eat

them. I've been up here since the storm started and so bogged down with corpses, I'm feeling like a haunt." Jeff Glory sagged against the near wheel. "You stare at them, Judge, but they just lay there. They ain't hungry."

"Y-you didn't—" Yontz began, aghast.

"Thought of it," admitted Jeff, "but couldn't decide. No bounty." He shook his head until his teeth clicked.

"You could have come back to Pineville," Yontz stated, "when Doc Neston's deputies broke through."

"Deputies?" Jeff hooted. "Body snatchers, you mean. I hadda fight them off." He groaned. "They stole my horses."

"Never mind now," soothed the judge. "Where are you camped?"

The liveryman, sacking dragging, staggered off. He had shoveled a path to the wall. On a level above his wagon he had poked a hole through the snow and built a fire. The wagon was almost used up, and he had covered the bodies with snow. Icicles dripped from the remaining canvas.

"You help me get them into Prescott?" Jeff crowded against his smoking fire. It sounded a forlorn request.

"On a two-horse buckboard? In this snow?

Leave them here. We'll drop over the summit and find you another team."

"No chance!" Jeff refused quickly. "If I leave them for a single minute, they'll be stolen. I never got no breaks before, Judge. That is, not until Marshal Tibbs gave those corpses to me. I'll make it come out right this time." He lowered his eyes and asked, "My bougainvillaea? Did it die with the first frost?"

"If it didn't, it went with the fire."

"Fire?" Jeff Glory's gloom deepened. "My barn burn? I knew it was that when I seen the smoke. I said to myself, 'That's the livery stable.' "

Judge Yontz was at a loss. The stableman was a real Jonah. Bad luck had driven this gentle Southern remittance man out of New Orleans. He had drifted west, failing at a hundred endeavors. Pineville had finally harbored the luckless man. When the Gobal gang had killed Omar Clay, Jeff Glory moved into the stable. No wonder Jeff was willing to fight for the pair of corpses and the expected bounty money.

"You've had it rough," Jeff," Yontz began, then stepped back with astonishment. Jeff Glory was training a heavy Sharps on the judge's midriff. It was close quarters for a long-barreled gun. Yontz moved to one side, and the rifle exploded. Its slug shattered the ice and sprayed chips onto the judge's collar. When the crash of the gun died, an uneasy silence filled the icy closet.

Jeff Glory's eyes were wild. He had fired on a Federal judge. Self-pity puckered his cracked lips as his shoulders slumped, and the hands holding the weapon began to tremble. "You—you understand, Judge? If I don't get them in, I got nothing left. My stable's burned, my horses stolen, even my vines is dead. . . ."

"Damn your vines!" snapped the judge. "If I don't get into Prescott before the marshal breaks those guerrillas out—"

"So you've turned on the marshal?" Jeff hissed. Now he could feel like a hero and protect the marshal. He frowned judicially. Yontz deserved to be stranded here. "Then you ain't going nowhere. I'm taking your wagon."

Judge Yontz knew he had said the wrong thing. This gun-happy pegleg had already gone too far to back down. The judge tried logic. "Look, Jeff, you can't get both bodies on that buckboard and still get out. The snow's too deep."

Jeff Glory was suddenly lighthearted. "A person's gotta keep trying. Ain't that right, Judge?" He moved the rifle muzzle against Yontz's belt buckle. "Don't you worry none. There's some wood left, and I'll tell folks where I left you."

"I'll just bet you will," grumbled the captive.

Minutes later Judge Yontz stood at the entrance of the snow cave and forlornly watched as Jeff Glory, both corpses tied snugly between the snow-clogged wheels, whipped the horses toward the exit of Crater Pass.

Fish-hunter hunched down against the wall around the Sasabe Plaza. The richly colored serape was loose around his shoulders, leaving a small roll to conceal his chin. Tibbs had been right. This Mexican border town was full of Anglos—tall, swaggering men from the North. Matamores, during the war, had seen such men. Gunrunners who manned freight wagons. Confederate soldiers sent across the border to transship supplies to the beleaguered South.

There was some difference today. These *Americanos* were waiting, marking time. Local gossip was a garbled history of their movements. Some months before they had crashed across the border. Their horses were lame, they were weary, and many wore bandages. They were not Westerners. The soft notes of border natives were not on their lips. These fighters, and many recognized that they were professionals, spoke slowly but with a harsh twang. Their leader, with a small escort, had continued south. It was believed he would rendezvous with Maximilian himself.

Meanwhile, Fish-hunter had been told that the colonel's men were waiting in Sasabe. They rested and they patrolled, staying south of the line but staring hungrily to the north. Mexicans who pretended to understand the Anglos were sure they recognized both homesickness and worry. It was believed by the Mexicans that these men had come a long way and that some of their compadres had been left behind.

Fish-hunter waited impatiently. The marshal had said, "Find Colonel Gater Grey. We'll need him at Barrel Wells." Fish-hunter scowled. Mexico was a huge place to search, but time was running out. The men were here in Sasabe, but where the devil was Colonel Gater Grey?

The web spun out in Pineville, sending its strands out over the territory. Marshal Tibbs was leading Captain Murphy's column across Grass Lake and soon would be marching them into Apache camp. Sid Peel, who had used the new route through the wild Tooloons, was galloping along the trail to Yuma. The desert grapevine had whispered that Piper Garfield, his two-week spree completed, was heading back to the PG Ranch. Piper had horses to spare, and Sid guessed that Piper would remember his promise to provide mounts for the column, but first he had to locate the rancher.

The marshal, Sid was positive, would get Captain Murphy's column out of the mountains and into the flatlands. But the border was still a long march away. If the plan failed, the territory from the mountains to the border was in for a full-scale bounty war. Doc Neston's posse had reached the burned-out stockade. They had made a forced march, and it was a disappointment. Snow had covered the column's tracks and gathered over the smoking ruins of Dixiecity. Proof of a hurried exit was everywhere. Saddles burned beyond use and stocks of carbines still smoldered.

"It ain't such a surprise," grumbled Doc Neston. "We knowed they was planning to leave." He was faced with a rebellious crew. Most of these men had spent weary days on Crater Pass camped in the snowdrifts. The few hours they had spent in Pineville saloons had lifted their spirits, but the tiring trek into the Tooloons had honed their tempers to a savage edge.

Fred Wade moved alongside Doc Neston. He

glared over the men like a hooded cobra as the spurs of shifting men tinkled. Many wolfish eyes glared back. They were not the stripe to be overawed. Their professional skill was only profitable with wanted men under their sights. If Wade could point out the bounty trail, they would follow.

"We've been snookered," Fred Wade admitted. "We're holding four aces with a cent pot. These guerrillas've been helped out of here. That double-dealing Marshal Tibbs got here first." He paused while curses and comments were passed around.

"An' how do we get into an honest game?" It was a man wearing a flat hat and a black bullhide coat who asked the question.

"We take out the crooked dealer," answered Wade. His voice was raised. "I am authorized by the governor to meet emergencies. We'll just sweeten the pot." He began to bark out his words. "The Territory of Arizona is now offering *five* hundred dollars for the capture—dead or alive— of Marshal Orion Tibbs!"

"Oh, sure you do," the black-coated man rasped. "Now whyn't you tell us where we're about to locate this walking gold mine?"

"Exactly! Somewhere between Crater Pass and the Mexican border." Wade held the eyes of his tormentor until the man ducked. He went on: "Now let's mount up and get along."

"Sure we will," another querulous voice said. "It's just like catching a whale in an arroyo. You just got to find the right puddle!"

12

Marshal Tibbs leaned out over the flooded ravine to judge the depth of the water. Boulders,
smashing along the bottom, growled as they
thumped past. Normally it was a dry wash, but
now the melting snow was cascading through the
steep banks.

The ravine had to be crossed. To follow it down
would drop them onto the Prescott road south of
the Pass where it dropped onto the flatlands.
Orion was sure, once Doc Neston discovered that
Dixiecity was destroyed, the bounty hunters
would hurry to cross over Crater Pass.

If the column followed this torrent, they would
find themselves under the waiting guns of Doc
Neston's crew. Crossing here was their only
chance. This trail led into Apache camp and then,
by easy stages, descended the far slope.

The worst of the snow-piled canyons were behind them. Captain Murphy's column, lugging
their fifty-pound packs, had tramped all night.
With Sergeant Rosser, Orion had scouted ahead.

Now here, a good two thousand feet lower in elevation, the melting snow had prepared a formidable barrier. To delay until the water subsided would mean several days lost. This retreating column couldn't afford to lose even an hour.

Sergeant Rosser, muddied to the waist, led his horse along the bank. "She's rougher than a cob. No horse can swim it, and no man is gonna jump it." He grinned hopefully. "Not unless we can figure some way to make it in two jumps."

Orion answered in kind. "It's about twenty feet. The first jump would put a man right in the middle. *Then* what?"

"Then," Rosser answered drily, "when we reach the flatland, we'd dig his body outta the muck."

The sergeant's joke promoted an idea. Orion pointed to a scraggly pinion tree. "Suppose we tie onto that tree and winch a rope across."

"If we get some men across," speculated Rosser, "we could make a flatboat, just big enough to haul our iron and the howitzers."

"Why the fifty pounds of iron?" Orion asked.

"If the captain didn't tell you"—Rosser grinned until the dark gums showed above his yellowed teeth—"why're you asking me?"

Orion tried again. "The captain said it was firepower."

The sergeant retained his low-lidded, noncommittal stare. Orion shrugged it off. It was obvious that Sergeant Rosser wasn't talking.

Mounting Mick, Tibbs yanked the dally string off his rope, looped it around his waist, and handed the loose end to Rosser.

"No horse can make that, Marshal!" Rosser was startled.

Patting Mick's neck where the mane bunched, Orion nodded his agreement. "It's those two jumps you talked about. One for Mick and the other for me."

The grizzled guerrilla was respectful. "You'll lose your horse for sure."

"Mick's hard to lose," Orion said quietly. "He might even make it all the way across."

"If you go under?" asked the awed sergeant.

"Then fire a salute as I go by." Orion backed Mick against the brush, kicked loose his stirrups, then spurred Mick forward.

Mick pranced and made a half turn. Orion felt the withers lower as the stout legs bunched to sprint. Mick took three powerful lunges, collected himself, and jumped.

For one wild second Orion thought Mick would make it. Sergeant Rosser let out an excited yell. But the muddy torrent was a full five feet too wide. Mick, his front hooves pumping for a solid base, hit only water. Orion raised and pushed himself strongly forward; he sailed over the horse's head, catching a fleeting glimpse of Mick's bugging eyes and puffing cheeks.

Orion grabbed for the pinon. The rough bark cut his hands as the powerful current tore at his torso. He clung for a second, then pulled himself up onto the far bank. Swiftly he turned to look.

Mick, his withers churning, his ears perked, his muzzle still above the surface, was disappearing downstream.

Sergeant Rosser threw Orion a look of sympathy and shouted, "That crazy horse thought he could make it!"

Working the dismantled howitzers over was a real task. The raft of green wood was loggy. Lean, cold men, roped to lifelines, fought the current. They guided the overburdened flatboat, swinging it against the far bank, then muscled the heavy pieces onto solid ground.

The rough boat was winched back and forth until the heavy packs were whipped across. The supplies came next—Ben Bolt's bacon, soggy flour, and the rock-hard beans. Captain Murphy, kneeling down to windward of a mesquite fire, watched his men with glum pride. Behind him the horses—Orion's pack animals, the Neston saddle mounts, the emaciated guerrilla animals—nibbled at the soaked branches of the bitter spruce.

When the last of the supplies had been ferried over, Orion Tibbs made the return trip to join the captain at the fire.

Captain Murphy raised somber eyes. "No way we can get those horses over?" They both knew the answer. The rest of the trek, until they reached Piper Garfield's spread, would be on foot.

Orion totaled it up. "The beans, bacon, and flour we can carry. Horsemeat, no. There's plenty of good grazing lower down. I'll work the horses lower." For a second his eyes clouded. "Mick—will be expecting me."

The captain understood. "I'll send Sergeant Rosser with you. And Marshal, I hope your horse made it."

"I figure he did." Orion nodded firmly, then went on, "You're right on the route to the Apache camp. There are hogans"—he smiled ruefully—"and even a corral. Carry your howitzers on a pole sling. Wait a full day. If the sergeant—or I—doesn't come back, drop down to Barrel Wells. My two deputies are sort of 'point' men. Sid's locating horses, and Fish-hunter is down in Mexico trying to find your brigade. Understand, Captain?"

"Understood, Marshal." Captain Murphy

watched Orion Tibbs and Sergeant Rosser ride off. Tibbs, he decided, was pure sinew and seasoned like oak with muscle fleshed over springy bone. The marshal's wide forehead, now smeared with mud, held a brain as intricate as a fine instrument. The man had reflexes like a puma. And what, the captain wondered, would be Tibbs's fate? He sighed. A lawman deliberately leading a column of wanted men to the safety of the Mexican border? Captain Murphy was beginning to understand the deep complexities of the other man. Tibbs had his own code. He didn't fret about what the law said. With men like this Pineville marshal, they did what they instinctively *knew* was right.

"Up and at it, Captain." The men on the far bank were grinning. "Time to get your feet wet!" Murphy, with a soft chuckle, twisted the tow rope around his waist and entered the savage water.

13

Judge Yontz spent the long night in Jeff Glory's snow cave atop Crater Pass. The fire had smoked, and what flame there was melted just enough ice to make a mess of the ground. Yontz curled as close to the fire as he could, and spent the hours dissecting the queer legal dispute that had burst over the territory.

The issues still confounded his legal mind. The trouble enfolding Pineville, leading to Max Rosser's murder and Wesley Neston's death, had pyramided from a single base. That stupid governor, he angrily mused, had mixed a mess of lethal mortar. True, all the building blocks had been present. The Rebels at Dixiecity, unemployed bounty hunters on the border, and, of course, Marshal Orion Tibbs at Pineville. Yet, Yontz had to admit, the main catalyst setting off the explosion was the new governor's bounty money. Two hundred dollars per Rebel!

Doc Neston had quickly moved in. The burly giant from Texas had taken command, insisting his brand be used and his corral would hold the captives. To Neston it was all a licensed manhunt; a Dixiecity massacre. It was gold, not justice, guiding the man hunters.

Tibbs, an ex-Yuma convict, paroled into Yontz's custody and later pardoned for his successful assault against the lawlessness, had recognized that the governor was stirring a brew of death. The marshal had tried to wet-sack the fire. Even now he was leading the intended victims to the safety of the distant border.

In his cold, snow-shrouded cell atop Crater Pass, Judge Yontz found himself hoping Tibbs would make it. Of course, Federal troops were duty bound to prevent such an escape. And Yontz stubbornly intended to alert those troops to prevent the escape. Tibbs would be caught in the middle. Military laws would smash the marshal— Yontz winced. Without Tibbs's exploding Colt, what would happen to Pineville and the wild Tooloon country? More drifting killers? A hole-in-the-wall to protect every criminal in the territory?

If it weren't so cold, Yontz could wait it out right here on the pass. The weather would ease, and the winter bunch grass would cover the ground. If the guerrilla column found safety across the border or—

He sat up and listened hard. The jingle of harness and the creaking of chill-tightened wheels were on the wind. Had Jeff Glory reconsidered and returned? Yontz hurried, slipping and sliding, back to the corduroyed section.

Doc Neston, as bulky as ever in a heavy sheepskin, led a trail-weary crew of horsemen. Several riders had knotted their ropes onto the wagon tongue to help the team drag the heavy cookwagon.

Raising a hand, Doc Neston urged his horse on. The men leaned forward on tired horses to stare at the Pineville judge. "Damned if it ain't the judge!" Doc's heavy lids lifted, and his white breath congealed in the frosty air.

"In person." Yontz managed a shaky grimace that he hoped could be construed as a smile of welcome.

Fred Wade moved his horse past Neston. "We'll take him along, Doc," he stated with authority.

Neston, tongue in cheek and enjoying the situation, asked, "You putting bounty on the judge?" Neston's tone implied that something had crawled from under a rock and should be stepped upon.

Fred Wade, sulky and bitter, replied, "The governor just might do that."

Feeling like a snowman standing numb while being pelted with snowballs, Yontz came to and demanded, "Bounty? For what?"

"Smuggling Tibbs and his deputies out of town," Wade sneered. "They call it aiding and abetting a conspiracy to defeat justice. It's against the best interests of the territory to assist in the escape of wanted men."

"Wanted men?" Yontz began, and was cut off when Wade kneed his horse forward until Yontz had to dodge.

"I'm talking," Wade snarled, "so you keep quiet until I finish! I was going to say, the governor leans pretty hard on a judge who protects the lawbreaker."

Judge Yontz slapped his hands together. He stuck his jaw forward and stomped his feet in the snow. Finally, through fury-gritted teeth, he snapped back, "Lawbreakers? Every damned deputy in what you call 'your posse' is a wanted killer!"

"Who says?" Doc Neston thrust his face down to confront Yontz.

"Aw, let's get over the pass." Fred Wade broke up the argument. "Do your fighting down where it's warmer."

"Get on the wagon; we'll cook it out of you tonight," Doc shouted, and drove his horse ahead.

The weary posse, knowing that Yontz's accusation had been close to the truth, sullenly followed.

Judge Yontz backed away to let the riders pass. He stepped forward as the cookwagon neared. The chalk-faced driver, whip in hand, flicked a nod toward the rear. Yontz climbed over the tailgate. Leaning back against a sack of flour, he braced himself and looked around. It was well stocked with a full sack of pinto beans, half a beef wrapped in sacking, and the usual iron cooking utensils. Several bottles of vanilla and three full jugs of Red Mountain whiskey were stacked around a full keg of black powder. Doc Neston, mused Judge Yontz, was supplied for a long hunt.

It grew warmer as they dropped below the snow level. When they reached the sloping foothills, they could look out on the distant flatlands of sand, cacti, and sandstone. Arroyos were rimmed with willows. In the clouded light the colors were still bright. Mostly green in tone against gray, they were backed by a horizon of a mysterious shade of bluish gold.

They made camp on a small shelf protected by wind-bent spruce. Men, asleep in their saddles, were prodded awake to dismount, walked only a few feet, then spread out on the leaf-matted ground. The cook, grousing but hurrying, soon had coffee boiling.

Judge Yontz, bone-chilled, moved to the fire. Doc Neston and Fred Wade were deep in conversation.

"Plotting the revolution?" quipped Yontz, and Wade glanced at Neston and shook his head. It was a negative signal, barely discernable.

The cook pushed forward. He waved a long-handled fork and shoved the tines close to Yontz's stomach. "You keep away from my cook fire," he ordered.

Judge Yontz drew back and walked away. This was a camp of bitter, sordid men. They had followed Doc Neston on a wild-goose chase all the way into Dixiecity, and they were tired. Where had the guerrillas gone? These bounty hunters survived by stealth, hunting down unsuspecting victims. Enticed by promises of easy money, they had joined Doc Neston, but the campaign had proved discouraging. Captain Murphy had blasted their camp in the grove, so might he not try another surprise attack? Were *they* now the hunted? It was an unpleasant thought to contemplate as they stared into the brush-covered slopes. The muzzles of those vicious howitzers might be aimed right down their throats.

Judge Yontz surveyed the camp. It was well protected, away from the cold wind that would blow down from the snowfield as night fell. Doc

Neston and Wade were still in deep conversation. He watched the pair finally part, and Fred wade sauntered over.

"As a favor to yourself, Judge, you'd better tell me just where Tibbs expects to take them Rebs." Wade sounded sympathetic, like a man readying to shoot an injured horse.

The judge answered with another question. "Will you hold off Doc Neston and his mad dogs?" Fred Wade was shaking his head as Yontz went on: "Can you arrange for the troops to round up the guerrillas?"

"There ain't no chance, Judge." Both were silent until Wade grunted softly. "Then you'd better be able to take it." He walked to the cookwagon and shoved a few hot biscuits into his pocket. In a matter of minutes he had ridden out of camp. Doc Neston watched him go and caught Yontz's eyes. Doc seemed highly pleased.

Before supper was finished, the rising wind brought a sprinkle. The bounty hunters had filled tin plates with beans and beef, then sought the protection of the close-limbed trees. They held low-voiced conversations and kept their attention on Doc Neston.

When the big man finished his meal, he slid his plate into the washtub and rummaged inside the cookwagon. He emerged with a whiskey jug, and the men quickly joined him at the fire.

Judge Yontz, watching with a jaundiced eye, remained under the larger spruce. Had Wade's sarcastic remark been a warning? What was Yontz expected to "take"?

The demijohn passed from hand to hand. The bounty hunters, torpid and exhausted only a few hours ago, frolicked and whooped. The rain gathered on their whiskery faces, catching reflections from the fire. They drank and threw razor-sharp glances over the raised jug in the direction of Judge Yontz.

When the jug had been drained to the last sloshing drop, Doc Neston began to rabble-rouse his crew. "When we left Texas's wide plains and rode north into the brush-covered rock country, we was promised the cooperation of the Territorial Law. The governor himself—" he gave the nearest man a push—"was standing as close as you are right now when he promised us such cooperation. And let me tell you, if we'd received it, we'd a had them Rebs." He glared around slowly until he reached Judge Yontz with his eyes. "And every man here woulda been going back to Texas with better'n a year's wages!"

"Amen, Doc—that's right!" a drunken voice

erupted. "Doc's sayin' it right out. We coulda had it. . . ." He turned morose. "Coulda had it 'ceptin' that dirty Arizona marshal done us out of it!"

"We're *still* going to bring them in, and don't you forget that!" Doc Neston shouted. "We'll find them. They're afoot, ain't they? Walking on them big Missouri bunions? They've gotta come outta these mountains. And they gotta get across that border, don't they?"

"Sayin' ain't catchin'," blurted the dirty man in the spotted sheepskin.

"Don't preach no sermon, Doc. Just show us the way," the first man was shouting. "We could use a good ol' Mississippi blue-tick hound. He'd sniff 'em out."

"We've got us a hound," Doc answered, and pointed to Judge Yontz. "He ain't exactly a blue tick; I'd say he's more like a legal beagle! But he knows where Tibbs's taken them Rebels. Bring him on over here." He turned to yell at the cook, "An' you fetch that extra keg of powder." Doc Neston smacked a huge fist against the flat of his hand. "We already had us our drink and our sermon. Now let's get down to the *real* entertainment."

Judge Yontz, hustled to his feet and dragged to the fire, almost panicked. Here in the dark, on the slope of this wet mountainside, Doc Neston was in full charge. Neston, diabolically tuning the temper of this nest of ruthless man hunters, could extol a terrible vengeance. Back at Pineville, Neston had swallowed his fury when he was told of Wesley Neston's death. The glare of hatred in those burning eyes had warned that he would seek revenge. Yontz's senses were sharply heightened to his present danger. He was alone in this scorpion's nest. Far below echoed the sounds of a flash flood rolling rocks through a steep dry wash. How many victims had screamed for mercy under those same conditions?

"Set him on that keg," directed Doc, and Yontz shivered. Neston *was* drunk. The craggy face, framed by firelight, was wet with a film of sweat and rainwater. The deep-set eyes glittered as if his brain were running ahead of the moment.

"Put him here—put him here." Doc staggered, and one boot slipped into the ashes. He pulled back and gave the judge a shove. Falling, Yontz was caught by rough hands and seated on the powder keg.

Reversing his Colt, Doc Neston hammered the plug free. The black powder dribbled out. Horrified, Judge Yontz watched it spread only inches from the fire.

"Now, Your Honor, you listen close." Doc had

to bend to glare unsteadily into his victim's face. "I'm just gonna ask you one question, one time. Only once, you hear? If I don't get the right answer, you're gonna ride into hell aboard that powder keg!" He leaned far back and banged his hands together.

"Which way out of these mountains is Tibbs taking them Missouri guerrillas?"

14

Orion Tibbs and Sergeant Rosser had to work
their horses higher up the slope to avoid being
trapped by the eroding banks of the flooded arroyo. The extra animals, including the under-
nourished bulls that the column had intended to
use as meat, moved listlessly ahead. An updraft
blew over fresh grass. The weary animals sniffed
the wind and needed little urging.

The arroyo, still a torrent clogged with debris,
dropped lower in a series of widening bends.
Orion knew its general direction. It would cut its
way, slowing as it descended, then finally flow out
well below Crater Pass in an alluvial sweep. If
Mick had survived this first severe descent, he
might have located a haven where the wash widened.

"Most horses would try to climb that wall," the
sergeant offered. Before Orion could reply, Rosser
discarded his tact. "But that hoss you got, he's a
thinker. He'd know to stay in the middle and wait
until the bank flattens out. He'd keep his legs off

the bottom, else those rolling boulders might hurt him bad. That about what you figure he'd do, Marshal?"

"He went under," Orion answered. "That current gets stronger as it gets deeper. Mick's got to stay away from the banks and off the bottom. He's going to get bumped on the bends. I guess he'll ride it out. We'll likely find him floundered down on the flat where it spreads out." Outwardly Orion was serene, but they both leaned anxiously forward to see around each sweeping turn.

The rage of these flash floods was awesome. Cattle, caught and flung along by the savage surge, were found later, bags of battered flesh and splintered bone. Those who rode it out and stayed alive usually had to be shot because of broken limbs. Mick was smart, but he was also flesh and blood and very vulnerable.

Orion remembered his last sight of Mick. The ears rotating, the muzzle, every whisker alert. Inwardly he cursed himself. Like Sergeant Rosser, he, too, had believed Mick might make that jump safely. He had simply been around that cocky horse too long.

The day passed slowly. Long before dark they passed a shallow mesa. It was heavily covered with second-growth timber after an ancient burn. Buckbrush was scattered and framed by bunch grass. Last year's grass had died, but the fresh green of new grass peeked through. Setting the spare animals loose, the worried pair dropped lower. As dusk was enveloping the canyon, they reined in.

Orion, by dead reckoning, believed they were ten miles, or the first three thousand feet, below the Crater summit. The water had risen and was now ebbing into the underbrush. It was a good sign. They hadn't seen anything of Mick, so he must be ahead. Dead, he would most likely have snagged on one of the driftwood-clogged bends. Alive, he would be flailing on, head bravely held high but becoming mighty weary.

"There's the Prescott stage road," Orion explained. "It's a bridge over this wash. I'll follow it down. Below, on the flat, all this mud and debris will be spread out. If there's a horse out there, he'll need help quick." He pointed upward. "Sergeant, you scout up higher. Neston's been to Dixiecity and now could be hurrying over Crater Pass. He—"

"Captain Murphy's orders was to stay with you." Rosser was blunt. A bottlefly buzzed in the brush; wind moaned in the treetops. Orion remained silent. Sergeant Rosser firmly added, "It can't be helped, Marshal."

"Without Mick, your column would never have crossed this wash!" Orion blazed.

"Mick's a horse," Rosser replied stubbornly. "He'll make out."

"Out here," Orion coldly snapped, "a man will do a lot to save a horse!"

"In Missouri, we'd do more to save the men we fight with."

The silence grew. Orion studied this sergeant who had already lost four sons. There was no give in the whiplike frame. He intended to follow his orders, even to using one of those heavy navy Colts. Killing Rosser wouldn't locate Mick. Captain Murphy would still try to fight his way across the flatlands into Mexico. With those deadly mountain howitzers and the extra iron, the column would leave a trail of wounded and dead.

Sergeant Rosser cut into Orion's thoughts. "There's something up there," he said softly, jerking his thin neck toward the stage road.

Orion listened. He heard the usual sounds of creaking branches, sighing wind, and the surge of swift water in the ravine.

"Sniff," Rosser urged.

Orion drew in a deep breath. The smell of roasted meat rode in on the breeze. Rosser was pointing. Leaning back, Orion could make out a gash in the overhang. That was the Prescott-Pineville road.

"The governor's deputies?" Rosser had lowered his voice, but his words were razor-sharp.

Nodding, Orion dismounted. He would have to abandon the search for Mick. Doc Neston wasn't stupid; he would have posted scouts and sent men on ahead to comb for Murphy's column. Or would he believe he was ahead of the guerrillas? That they were afoot and trying to slip over the pass? If so, why had he brought his men this far down the southern slope? Afraid of Murphy's howitzers in the narrow pass? A hundred guerrillas, fighting for their lives, would be a tough crew to box in. Doc Neston's best bet would be to hurry ahead and set up an ambush on the flatlands. In the open and mounted, the Neston crew could split the column like a pool shark, and once scattered, they could be hunted down. Mounted men would have a pig-sticking bounty hunt.

"Best get on back?" Rosser suggested.

Tibbs shook his head. "If they locate Mick, they'll be able to backtrack us. We'll ease up there and do some scouting of our own." Leading his horse, he angled up the slope. Without a word, Rosser followed.

Night was swift, but they reached the road in

the first gloom. They pushed into the buckbrush and anchored the horses. The manzanita grew tall, and they edged around the shiny trunks. Flames from a large campfire outlined the camp.

Doc Neston's crew had gathered at the fire. Beyond was the cookwagon where the dour cook was busy with his housekeeping. The fragrant smell of cooked meat had evaporated, replaced by the pungent smell of raw whiskey. It was the bounty hunters. Fifty or more men jostled around the fire. Their horses stomped in a corral made of knotted ropes.

Orion straightened, looking down on the gathering. Doc Neston raised his head and swung his eyes over the area; as he again bent down, Orion heard him shout, "You'll tell us, Yontz, or you'll go up like a skyrocket!"

The group parted, and Orion made out the shock of white hair above the flushed face. Yontz was seated on a small powder keg. They had tied his hands so tightly behind his back, his plump stomach jutted out. His jowls were quivering with anger.

"We'll give him a touch," Neston ordered. A man hefted a cup and dribbled a stream of powder away from Yontz's feet. Doc, waving a burning stick, applied the flame to the trail of powder.

It smoked a moment, caught with a puff, and raced across the ground.

At Orion's shoulder Sergeant Rosser released a deep breath to mutter, "They're goin' to blow him up!"

Before Orion could move, the trail of fire reached the victim's feet. It jolted the judge and smoked along the nap of his woolen pants. His face was gray, but his lips were set. Doc Neston, weaving, leaned down to shout into the stoical face, "There's a sample! Now, where'd Tibbs take them Rebels?"

The click of a hammer drew Orion around. Sergeant Rosser was taking a bead on Doc Neston. Orion reached around and clamped a hand over the breech, hammer, and cylinder. If Rosser triggered, the meat of Orion's thumb would take the pin, but the cartridge wouldn't explode. Their eyes locked.

Orion whispered sharply, "That won't work. They'd still kill the judge. Put it away." He motioned toward the corral. "I'll work over behind the remuda, cut the rope, and stampede them through the fire."

Rosser nodded easily, and Orion lifted his hand from the guerrilla's weapon.

"You snatch the judge, Sergeant. Hurry him

back to where we left the horses. Wait there." He started to move toward the corral. The men at the fire jerked around; several flashed a hand to their waist guns.

A man leading a bedraggled Mick rode in. He was a half-breed, his black hair knotted into a bun, Zuni-style. The wide-brimmed hat set straight on his proud head. Orion's eyes checked Mick. The saddle was scarred, the leather wet and ripped. Mick had a knot on his brisket and a gash along the withers. He sagged, leaning to the right, and Orion guessed that his left front leg was injured. His head and barrel neck drooped, but his whiskers and ears were as pert as a colt's.

"Now's the time to move!" Orion whispered, and bending double, he raced for the remuda. He slashed the rope passing between the startled animals and began to fire his six-gun. The leaders, crowded by those behind, broke for the campfire.

Orion caught a glimpse of Sergeant Rosser, who had hoisted Yontz onto his shoulder and crashed back into the brush. Orion circled the excited men and came up on the off side of the Indian. He pulled the man down, cracked the gun butt against his temple, and let him drop. Mick nickered. Orion caught the rein and led him off. At the edge of the road he looked back. The fire had been scattered. Shapes of men staggered about in the dark. Doc Neston had found his voice. "Let the damned horses go! Pull back to the cook-wagon. We're about to be attacked!"

15

Captain Murphy's column was settled in at the Apache camp. Fires smoked in the lee of the hogans. Beans, flavored with bacon, boiled in clay pots left by the Indians. Marshal Tibbs, Sergeant Rosser, and Judge Yontz were gathered in Captain Murphy's hogan.

Judge Yontz, weary and bruised, still managed to pace the small room. The discussion had been going on for several hours. For the fifteenth time Yontz repeated, "Captain, you've got to take your men in to surrender. There are Federal troops at Prescott, and they'll treat you like soldiers."

Wearily Captain Murphy looked into the patient eyes of the marshal before whirling on Judge Yontz. "But your government's bounty has already signed our death warrants!"

"Listen to me!" Yontz's fury matched the stubborn calm of the captain. "The governor's authority extends only to civil matters. It does *not* extend to Rebel soldiers who wish to surrender. *That* comes under the army's jurisdiction. Federal officers will not execute men who have surrendered. Don't you see? By running for the border, you're playing right into the governor's hands."

Captain Murphy sighed, extended a large hand, and gripped the judge's shoulder. Twisting the cloth of his shirt, Murphy drew Yontz forward and snapped, "My soldiers fought well. Our raids and cavalry attacks tied down Fremont's army. General Lane," he sneered, "who is now recognized here, was outfought. Then Lee surrendered, and suddenly we are no longer soldiers but renegades. If the war had been won by the South, our men would have been the heroes. Statues would have been raised to Quantrill and Mosby. Does the scratch of a pen turn a soldier into a renegade? As for your Federal army giving us protection, I'll not gamble one man—"

Yontz had jerked free and was shouting, "You talk of heroes and renegades and gambling! Face facts! You have a hundred men stuck halfway up on this mountainside. The Mexican border is a hundred miles away. You don't have horses. Doc Neston can range out on the flats and cut you to pieces. The men who escape will be hunted like wolves!" He halted, out of breath, and glared into Captain Murphy's stony eyes.

"Get on in and make a deal from strength! Ask for amnesty!" Yontz went on. "Do it before Fred

Wade gets to the governor. Before they indict you for firing your howitzers into Pineville!" Yontz resumed his pacing and turned his fury onto the silent marshal.

"And you, Tibbs, what have you done? You know this country. Without horses, how can they possibly reach the border?"

"They've come this far," began Orion, yet he knew the judge was advancing a fair argument. Back at Pineville, after the howitzer attack, Yontz had agreed that the guerrillas should try for Mexico. What had changed his mind? Now he was suggesting amnesty, surrender to the governor. The legal mind, Tibbs guessed, couldn't leave a problem alone. And the judge might be right, yet how do you convince an officer to surrender one hundred men? And the governor was already committed. He had placed the bounty and sent in Doc Neston with his man hunters. Captain Murphy was determined to go on. Orion could understand it; fight your way to safety or die on your feet! Yontz's way meant death from ambush or from the carbines of an army firing squad. Besides, at this juncture, could they trust the advice of a judge's complex reasoning?

All present were waiting for Orion's answer. Sergeant Rosser edged close. This marshal had be-

haved well so far. He had led them out of the beleaguered Dixiecity. If the storm had lasted a few
days longer, Doc Neston's crew would have remained trapped on the other side of Crater Pass.
Even without horses, the column might have out-
distanced pursuit. Both Captain Murphy and Sergeant Rosser were uneasy. Would the judge's
legal threats swing the marshal of Pineville?

Watching the pacing judge, Orion continued to
think it through. Had Sid Peel made contact with
Piper Garfield? Would Piper furnish the horses
for that last furious dash to the border? And Fish-
hunter? Had the stolid Indian reached Colonel
Gater Grey? Could this hustling column continue
the man-killing pace for another two days and stay
ahead of Doc Neston's man hunters? Then there
was Fred Wade. According to Yontz, the governor's gunman had ridden off, leaving the judge to
the mercy of Doc Neston. Might not Wade be
planning a flanking movement with army troops?
The thought gnawed at him. Had Wade somehow
guessed that Piper Garfield was supposed to furnish mounts?

It all added up to long odds against the column
reaching safety. They had no other choice but to
play out those odds. They would have to cut a cor-
ridor across the Arizona flatlands and fight their

way to the border. He gave his answer slowly in the tense room. "They've come this far, Judge. Seems to me they have to try for the border."

Judge Yontz's breath exploded.

Captain Murphy offered cheerfully, "You're welcome to join us, Judge."

"I'm afraid not, Captain." Yontz ran a shaking hand through his sweaty hair. "I never was much of a walker. 'Specially with a bounty-hunting army on my trail." He turned to Orion and with some spirit, muttered, "I'll drop back down to where we left the horses. Don't worry, I'll see that Mick gets good care."

"You're going on to Prescott?" Orion asked.

The judge gloomily nodded. "I have to. That blasted Jeff Glory's got my buckboard."

Captain Murphy issued his orders. "Sergeant, have the men prepare to march."

Prescott, Arizona Territory, was a black blob with a glow of light in the center. The solid citizens had built their homes well out from the honky-tonk Pioneer Square. It was past midnight; clouds hung low and threw gloomy shadows over the staggering dunes.

Sid Peel, his bandy legs braced under lugging the weight of Piper Garfield, kept to the edges of shadows. The dray wagon, its wheel rims wrapped

in gunny sacks, was following the lurching pair.
Piper's foreman, trapped into this nefarious
scheme, sat stolidly on the spring seat.

Sid had located the flatlands' cattle baron,
which had taken some hard riding. Piper, re-
nowned for the length of his periodic sprees, had
left Yuma, bypassed the home ranch, and headed
for Prescott. Sid had finally caught up with the
pair at a cantina ten miles out of town.

Piper had listened, downed his drink, and
agreed. "I can let you have the horses for those
Missouri boys." He had poured another drink,
then morosely added, "Some may be distant kin."

Sid had been grateful. When the marshal sent
him out to locate a hundred horses, it had seemed
a wild-goose chase. Crater Pass had been blocked.
Doc Neston's crew of bounty hunters had been
gathering in the grove below Pineville. Captain
Murphy's column was still dug in at Dixiecity.
Yet Tibbs's instinctive foresight, a sort of all-
seeing eagle's eye, had envisioned the escape of
the guerrillas from a trap at Dixiecity to the safety
of Mexico, half way across the Arizona Territory.
Sid breathed easier. It was working out.

Piper had downed a second drink and spoke
with smug humor. "Sid, where you going to locate
a hundred saddles?"

Sid stared. Piper was wide of shoulder, lean of

hip, and very tall. He favored a flat-topped black hat that made him look like a wedge ready to be sledged into the ground. Now there was a droll leer on his face. The question stumped Sid. Orion hadn't said a thing about bridles or blanket pads, and certainly nothing about saddles.

"Men can usually furnish their own riding gear," Piper bantered. "All we got is broncs. Some is buckjumpers or sunfishers, but most is plain, untamed hammerheads. How're your soldiers gonna stay atop them kind without gear?" He sneezed and gulped another drink. "Let ol' Piper tell you how. We're gonna borrow that gear from the quartermaster in Prescott!"

The foreman had agreed to go along, with the proviso that he stay with the wagon. They had borrowed a team of spavined horses, hitched up the wagon, and trotted into Prescott. At the edge of town Piper had drifted off, and Sid was walking the rancher awake.

"Hssst!" The foreman pointed to the warehouse. Sid proped Piper against the wall and scouted the building. It was deserted. No sentries, no watchman, just a barn-type building filled with army supplies. The foreman bent forward and answered Sid's unspoken question. "Freighter's storage barn. Quartermaster ain't accepted delivery yet. The tightwad skinner won't pay watchman's wages." He looked around nervously. "Open her up. Let's get in and get out!"

An hour later they were back on the road heading for the Garfield ranch. The wagon springs sagged as the team strained to keep the wheels from bogging down in the muddy ruts. Sid Peel was content. Enough gear to outfit Captain Murphy's men was packed under the canvas top. If Marshal Tibbs could walk the guerrillas out of the stormy Tooloons, they would be riding when they left Garfield's. Sid leaned back for a nap.

In the gray light before dawn the foreman nudged Sid awake. He pointed with the whip stock. They had reached the Pineville cutoff. A lone horseman, the Crater Pass heights looming behind him, was trotting toward them.

The foreman licked his lips. "I'll do the talking." He drew the tired horses to a halt and cautioned Sid, "Keep him covered. Night riders is always dangerous."

The rider reined in, and his horse, edgy at the sight of the ghostly canvas, danced sideways. The seven-pointed star caught the dull light, and the foreman greeted Fred Wade. "Heard you was in Pineville. Doc Neston's Texans collect all that bounty money yet?"

Wade ignored the taunt. "Who's with you? Piper Garfield?"

"Fetchin' him home," answered the foreman. "He's been on some dillies, but never one like this. Fidst off, he opened up Yuma until it was plumb wore out and—"

"Never mind." Wade was tired. "That little fellow . . . ain't I seen him before?"

"I don't know nothing about what they done," snorted the foreman. "I just hire them. Says he worked as a hay hand. Never can get too many hay hands."

Without a further word Fred Wade eased off the reins and broke into a trot toward Prescott.

Sid leaned out to watch Wade disappear, then shook his head. "Sure like to know what's been going on. That's the governor's hatchet man, and he's trouble."

"The way I hear it, your Marshal Tibbs got him bluffed and buffaloed." The foreman cracked his whip and kicked off the brake.

"Yeah." Sid holstered his Colt with a grin. "We really got him buffaloed."

16

With Orion Tibbs in the lead, Captain Murphy's column departed the Apache camp during the night. The old trail, widened over the years by the travois of the Indians, was fair-going. Murphy's guerrillas were rested and sniffed the free, surging wind up from Mexico. The howitzers were slung on poles, the shells lugged along on bent backs. This was their third night out of Dixiecity, and their gait quickened.

Reaching the stage road, Captain Murphy put out scouts and allowed a half hour's rest. The packed surface was muddied, and the scouts reported the tracks of a single horseman.

Satisfied that Doc Neston's man hunters were still rounding up their scattered horses, Orion led the column straight down the road. At dawn they rested for an hour before starting across the sandy wastes leading to Piper Garfield's home spread. By noon they had reached the Prescott cutoff where Fred Wade had met Sid Peel and his wagonload of saddles.

While Orion studied the wheel tracks, Captain Murphy led his column into the dunes. He returned with Sergeant Rosser. Both men's lean faces were pinched under the strain of another full night of enforced marching.

"We've come a good thirty miles today, Marshal," the captain stated.

"And another thirty to go to the Garfield ranch." Orion offered no sympathy.

"The men need rest, Marshal. They're cavalry, not infantry."

"I've heard, Captain, that cavalry are only mounted infantry. Now we're about to prove that. Doc Neston's men are behind us." He grinned at Sergeant Rosser. "As soon as they discover they aren't under attack, they'll begin putting the pieces together. Someone will remember that Mick is my horse. They'll scout around, and I'll bet you a dollar Neston's on the road somewhere behind us right now."

"But even the regular infantry can't outmarch cavalry!" Murphy snorted. Sergeant Rosser nodded agreement. "The men are carrying packs and howitzers, not to mention ammunition."

Tibbs answered solemnly, "A man fighting for his life can do more than he believes he can." He looked at the lowering sky and went on, "Get them on their feet. We'll be at the ranch by morning."

"But Neston's men are mounted—they'll catch us out in the open!" the captain argued.

"They just might do that," reasoned Orion. "However, he *won't* charge those mountain guns." He studied the officer's angry face, and his tone turned bantering. "You can still take the course Yontz offered."

Captain Murphy, stiff-backed, made a quick-paced turn and marched over to the dunes. Rosser clumped alongside Orion to mutter, "Thirty miles already and another thirty to go. Lord help us if those horses ain't there."

"On your feet, men!" Captain Murphy was ordering. "The howitzer crew will bring up the rear. Sergeant Rosser will assign a detail to support the gunners. The ranch, where our horses will be waiting, is another thirty miles." He raised one hand to still the protesting curses. "Fall in and follow the marshal." With groans, the guerrillas lined up.

His own legs stiff from the respite, Orion stepped past the ranks. Most of these men were lank, and those heavy with muscle were the exception. Years of hit-and-run fighting had leaned them out. Long-armed, gaunt-faced, with rawboned, almost skeletal features, their posture was still military. They had been farm boys once. The war had made them into skillful horsemen, noted for their ferocious firepower. Orion understood now why they cheerfully lugged the heavy packs. Each man was carrying six navy Colts.

Federal cavalry relied upon the Spencer carbine, which carried seven shots in the stock and one in the chamber. They also used the saber and a holstered Colt. But these guerrillas, holding the reins in their teeth, could fire thirty-six shots without reloading.

Doc Neston's men had plenty of rifles, which meant effective long-range power. But Captain Murphy's howitzers should keep them well out of range.

Orion was expecting a fight. He hoped it would wait until after they reached the Garfield ranch. Once mounted, these guerrillas need fear no pursuit. Neston's crew couldn't stand a Rebel charge, and would melt under the handgun fire of these guerrillas. Neston's best battlefield lay between these dunes and the ranch.

Orion thought about the tracks of the single rider. Judge Yontz had reported that Fred Wade had left the mountain camp alone. Wade, with his sinister intuition, might have guessed Orion's escape plan. The governor, deeply involved, would

furnish U. S. cavalry. This weary column had to
get on. A march through the afternoon and coming night was necessary to reach the Garfield
spread. Sid Peel would be waiting. Only then
could these rugged men, with the worst behind
them, mount up and ride on.

Somewhere between Sasabe and Barrel Wells,
Fish-hunter would bring on Colonel Gater Grey's
brigade. Crossing the border, which was guarded
by strong Federal patrols, would be the final problem. The army, forewarned, would saturate the
possible escape route. Doc Neston would be
hurrying along in the rear. Mexico was a large
country, but Orion believed Colonel Grey would
still be stationed in the northern province. Fish-
hunter had to locate the Missouri brigade, convince Colonel Grey, and lead the brigade back to
the border. Then, and only then, would a safe
crossing be insured for Captain Murphy's men.

Orion looked back and saw that the column
had found its stride again and were swinging
along. The problem right now was to get through
the afternoon without being located.

Dusk found them crossing a dead lava flow a
full mile wide. The rocks, sharp as glass, cut
through the worn leather of their boots. Men
stumbled and cursed, but the rising moon helped
them through. Again they single-filed past more

dunes and through more ravines. Trickles of water seeped along the bottoms, and willows gave them protection from the wind.

Two hours after dark they rested. The men hunkered down, chewed on dried bread, and stared toward the south.

With Sergeant Rosser following, Orion climbed a nearby dune and studied the horizon. The Tooloons, mantled by snow, were bulked against the black sky.

"They out there?" Rosser asked.

"They are," reasoned Orion. "For two hundred dollars a head they'll be coming on hard."

"I expect so. Are we going to make it to the ranch by morning?"

Turning his back to the mountains, Orion surveyed the land sloping away to the south. "Something doesn't fit," he grunted. "Doc Neston's mounted crew should have caught up before we reached the lava beds."

Rosser, uneasy, stared at the marshal of Pineville. "You was expectin' them? And you still kept right on? Whyn't we hole up at the lava flow and dig in where we could fight them off?"

"No chance. They'd hold us down and pick us off. We've got to get across that border."

"We'll do that real quick once we get aboard

them horses," boasted the sergeant. "There can't nothin' stop us."

"Nothing?" Orion was quizzical. He felt the mystery of the desert at night. Shadows for men to hide in. A soft wind that blew the wrong way. Sounds that carried in a dozen directions. He remembered the tracks at the crossroad. A single horseman who turned away from the wagon tracks. That had to be Fred Wade. Wade, the professional man hunter, could outmaneuver a coyote. A strong hunch suddenly came over Orion. Had Wade left Doc Neston's crew, not because they were preparing to torture Judge Yontz, but because he had some plan of his own?

Orion swung around to face the sergeant. Down there lay Mexico. In a direct line, fifty miles at the most, was Barrel Wells. A hundred men, with two mountain guns, could defend Barrel Wells until Hades froze over. Tibbs dug in his heels and scrambled off the dune.

Locating the captain, he flatly stated, "Our timing is off." He swiftly went on to explain his change in plans. The column would head directly south, bypassing the Garfield ranch, and dig in at Barrel Wells. They would be closer to the border and could hold until Fish-hunter arrived with Colonel Gater Grey's brigade. Sensing the captain's rising confusion, Orion added, "The governor's man, Fred Wade, might have it all figured out. Garfield's the only rancher in these parts. Maybe the only one in the territory with enough horses to mount your column. See?"

"Partly, Tibbs," admitted Murphy. "And you believe he might have Federal troops waiting at the Garfield ranch?"

"Troops *and* Doc Neston's men," Tibbs agreed. "That would be smart. You would walk right into an ambush. Out here the shoe's on the other foot. Your howitzers can hold them off."

Captain Murphy raised a weary head to protest, "But that's another fifty miles! Marshal, these men are dog-tired. This is the second night without sleep and—"

"A firing squad will put them to sleep forever," snorted the marshal. He stooped to draw a map in the sand. "You're here, Captain. Barrel Wells is right there." He slid his finger through the sand in a straight line. "You get going and you keep moving until you get there." His voice was taut. "Then you settle in and wait."

"And where are you going, Marshal?" Captain Murphy's voice had become resigned.

"I've got a deputy at Garfield's ranch," snapped Orion. "I don't intend that Wade or Neston'll stick any pins under his fingernails." Then he smiled to show his confidence. "Don't worry, Captain, you have a hundred fighting men and more firepower than a regiment!"

"Of course. We'll make it, Marshal." Captain Murphy rose and made a short bow, then reached out to shake Tibbs's hand firmly. "I sincerely trust you will find your deputy alive."

17

The last few hours before dawn were the worst. Tibbs had forced himself to keep moving since leaving the column. He had turned once to watch the snakelike shadow swing to the south. Some of the men staggered and a few reeled, but, pitching and swaying, the guerrillas had marched toward Barrel Wells.

As the sun lightened, the sandstone buttes sent widening shadows around the dunes, and Orion broke into a jolting trot. A moving object could be seen for miles on the desert surface, and he wanted to be close to the Garfield buildings before full sunup.

He circled to come up from a hayfield and had entered the tall, succulent grass when he heard the moan. A horse, saddled but with reins dragging, was munching the crisp fodder. Tibbs eased forward, raised an arm, and captured the reins. Startled, the horse jerked up his head and pulled back. "Whoa, boy, easy. . . ." Orion coaxed.

"That you, Marshal?" Sid Peel's voice squeaked

with pleasure. The deputy's peaked face rose out of the grass and he smiled, but his eyes were dull with pain and remorse.

Orion moved swiftly to the deputy's side. His right sleeve was ripped to the shoulder. Sid had used his kerchief to bind a bloody wound.

"I think the slug broke a bone," Sid offered, trying to wriggle his fingers.

"They shot you and left you here?" Tibbs asked with heat.

"It couldn't have happened no better," replied Sid quickly. "They seen me drop and figured I was finished."

"Who shot you—Doc Neston?"

Sid was puzzled. "Neston. No, it was Fred Wade. Come riding right in with maybe twenty troopers from Prescott. They found our saddles. Me and Piper made a bolt for it, but they caught him quick. You should've seen him quartering around the corral." Sid chuckled weakly. "With twenty men trying to catch him." He winced and positioned his arm to ease the pain. "It gave me a chance to jump the corral and cut out of there. But a tall trooper—maybe about seven feet tall and with an eye like Daniel Boone—cut me down with a sniper's rifle."

"Saddles?" Orion waited. You had to let Sid rave and then retrace to fill in the blanks.

Sid replied sheepishly, "It was a helluva good idea. Piper offered the horses right off. Then we had a few drinks and figured we'd better get some saddles. A hundred miles on a bare-backed mustang would cut a man into twins right up the middle!"

"So Fred Wade met you coming back from Prescott? You were using a dray wagon?"

"Yep, it was Wade. Sneaking around and putting it all together. He guessed why we wanted them saddles. So he just collected a squad of cavalry and rode down on the ranch."

"Piper Garfield helped you steal government property?" Orion was surprised. The most he had expected was a grudging loan of horses.

Sid hurried to answer, "It's all coming out about that carpetbagging governor! Right off he put that bounty on the guerrillas because *he's* taking a bite on every dollar to be paid out." Sid lowered the lid of one fretful eye. "It was Doc Neston worked it all out. He promised the governor twenty-five per cent." Sid spat. "That governor'd never stand a chance in an election, so he's getting it quick and getting out."

"And Piper Garfield?" Orion was patient.

"I think Piper's got his eye on the governorship. Anyway, he's roaring mad—the governor having men killed for profit and all." Before

Orion could comment, Sid rambled on, "You know how it all came out? The deal between Neston and the governor?"

Orion shook his head and nodded for Sid to go on.

"All because Jeff Glory brought in them two corpses you killed in Pineville. Proud as a road-runner, Jeff demanded his bounty money. It was promptly paid—less the governor's twenty-five per cent." Sid couldn't stifle a chuckle. "You understand, Orion? The governor thought Jeff was one of Doc Neston's men. Right? Well, you know Jeff. He sang to high heaven. Man gets his first real break and somebody steals twenty-five per cent. Doesn't that sound like Jeff? And who come into town right about then?" Sid's hysteria was building. "Judge Yontz! He's hot on Jeff's trail, anyway, because Jeff stole his buggy—"

"I see it all now," Orion soothed the excited deputy. And it did, he thought, make a grimly riotous picture. Yontz, when roused, was a spur-raking terror. The governor's double-dealing would fire the judge like a steam geyser. He would start pulling wires in Washington. He would shout and stomp until the citizens of the territory would join in. Action would follow, but too late, guessed Orion, to aid Captain Murphy's column. The governor, facing exposure, would hurry to drop the net. By sending Federal troops to raid the Garfield ranch, he had implicated the army for private gain. Yontz would have a field day with that sort of legal argument.

Sid had said that Doc Neston wasn't at the ranch. The bounty hunters, well mounted, would even now be trailing the footsore guerrillas toward Barrel Wells. Wade's ambush had failed. Sid was free.

"Sid." Orion gave his wounded deputy a slight shake.

"Eh?"

"There's a wash below here. I'll crawl down there, leading this horse. Then I'll come back for you. You get into Prescott, see a doctor, then tell Yontz what's going on out here. Wade's using troops for bounty hunting and Neston's trailing the column. Understand?"

"Sort of, but . . . ain't you going in there after Piper?"

Orion shook his head. Neston must be out of touch, hurrying along after the column and counting the dollars he would collect on each dead guerrilla.

The governor, back in Prescott, would be edgy. Yontz's rabble-rousing would be having an effect. Hurt once, the governor would be willing to believe the threat of another blow. There just might be a way, Orion speculated, to get Captain Murphy's men safely across the border.

Suppose Fish-hunter had run into trouble? Anything could happen below the border. Colonel Grey might refuse to cooperate. Hadn't he once left the column behind? Would the brigade dare to leave Mexico to fight a battle with Federal cavalry along the border?

It was risky, but Orion Tibbs decided to use any pressure available. It would be known in Prescott that Captain Murphy had already used his cannon on Pineville. Known also that the guerrillas were rugged raiders with the desperation of doomed men. Yontz, now divorced from his respect for the governor, would join in.

"Piper will make out," Orion answered Sid, and went on to explain. "You ride on into Prescott. Pass the word that Doc Neston was ambushed by Captain Murphy's column. Got that?" At Sid's nod, Orion continued: "Neston was flanked and wiped out. Make it sound good. That will give the column Neston's horses, so Murphy is heading for Prescott and is going to blow the town apart."

"Will that get them away?" queried the deputy.

"It might pull in the cavalry to protect Prescott. At least Fred Wade will be ordered back. If the patrols are brought in from the border, the column can get across without a fight."

"If they outrun Doc Neston!" Sid was wary. "It's a mighty long walk to Barrel Wells."

It had also been a laborious trek from the Apache camp, Orion mentally added. Bypassing Garfield's ranch had put on another fifty miles of enforced marching. Somewhere before the column could reach Barrel Wells, Orion knew that Doc Neston would catch up to the column. There would be a showdown fight, guerrilla versus bounty hunter. Orion Tibbs, marshal of Pineville, intended to be present.

18

Men who walk the desert alone enter a realm of unreality. They stumble along during the daylight and huddle close to some protective outcropping during the night hours. The coyotes call out, and small animals scurry about searching for food and dodging predators. The desert is cut by coulees, blocked by dead lava streams, and shadowed by bulking buttes. Fragrant creosote and greasewood tangle with mesquite.

Orion Tibbs, a full half day behind the fleeing column of guerrillas, jolted south. The recent rains had firmed the sand. New growth glowed in the faint moonlight. The wind rolled sand particles from the slopes. The washes, once dry, were soggy with mud. His tall bootheels hampered his stride. Small rocks tripped him and he staggered. Blisters broke and began to bleed. He thought longingly of Mick, now chomping hay in some Prescott corral.

Twenty miles out from Garfield's ranch, he crossed fresh horse tracks. Fifty mounted men

were heading dead-on for Barrel Wells. These had
to be Doc Neston's man hunters. Doc, coming off
the Crater Pass road, had read his signs well. He
had locked onto Captain Murphy's direction and
was following hard.

Orion climbed a sloping dune to stare out over
the area. The dead land was silent and nothing
moved. Far in the distance a pair of identical
buttes, like twins, rose from the flats. Orion staggered down the slope and moved on. Dawn found
him but two miles from the twin buttes. Soon Doc
Neston would cross the guerrillas' trail. The wind
would gather the dust kicked up by the weary
men. Hunters would send out flankers and—

The first shots rumbled as Doc Neston opened
his attack. Orion climbed a slope and could see
the fight. It was, in the half-light before dawn, a
ghostly battle unfolding against the glowing horizon.

Doc Neston had split his men into squads and
sent them straight out of the wash. Now Orion
could make out the guerrilla unit. They were
beyond the buttes, a crawling serpent on the next
rise. As he watched, the column snaked itself into
a defensive circle. A fight at the waterhole, except
that the center of this circle was dry sand and
rock. Where were the howitzers? Had the guerrillas abandoned them?

Neston's horsemen, keeping well out of revolver range, moved ahead slowly. Orion guessed
their intent: to lay back on the flanks and pick off
the defenders by rifle fire.

The crack of their rifles drifted back to Orion.
Drum fire, like hunters killing buffalo. Neston's
men were dismounting, chosing firing stands, and
pouring in the slugs.

Captain Murphy's column was digging in but
pinned down. Their handgun firepower was use-
less at that distance. Captain Murphy had hustled
his men across the last stretch, but they had fallen
short of Barrel Wells. There he would have held
the advantage. The pockmarked cliffs offered con-
cealment, and with those mountain guns . . .
Orion felt like swearing.

Neston's men were growing careless. Safely out
of short-gun range, they swaggered back and
forth. The squad on the right had found a new
high spot and began gathering there. The
riflemen on the far side were beginning to inch
forward. Orion wondered what sort of division
they had decided upon. Would they pool the
bounty or—? He erased that thought. Captain
Murphy was no fool.

Doc Neston's plan of battle was becoming clear.
The riflemen on the high point would pin down
the guerrillas while the others worked their way

closer. If a guerrilla raised himself up to fire, he would become a target for a long-range sniper. The day was beginning and many men would die before dark. With sundown, the odds would increase for Neston. His pitted riflemen could work a dangerous crossfire.

There was some movement on top of the twin buttes. The rising sun sparkled on metal. A puff of powder smoke rose, followed by a cough, as a canister left the howitzer muzzles. The pair of mountain guns had almost point-blank range. Their position was a bare two hundred yards from Neston's snipers and less from his rifle pits.

The pitmen, hearing the cannon blast, poked their heads up. The shot dropped close, and the jagged iron tore at the sand. A second shot was closer. Panic set in. Like a covey of quail, they scattered. The canister found several and they fell. Their bodies marked a line where the advance had been stopped.

The snipers, entrenched on the high point, held until the second round. Their sudden desire to retreat turned into a rout. Men leaped off the point and rolled down the sandy slope. Their horses, caught up in the excitement, broke free. Tails high, they galloped off the slope and disappeared.

The tide of battle had turned. Captain Murphy's gunners—Orion pictured Sergeant Rosser squinting down the stubby barrel—were real experts. In the next half hour both of Neston's squads, skirmishers and snipers, were completely routed. Captain Murphy's circle was safe as long as those howitzers commanded the slopes.

However, would Captain Murphy pull his howitzers back and continue his retreat toward Barrel Wells? Was he planning to wait for dark and sneak off? Orion was concerned. If the guerrillas scattered, they would be whittled down by the mounted man hunters. They had tried but could not outmarch Neston's horsemen. It was still a long ten miles to Barrel Wells. They had been saved by the howitzer fire, but those guns needed a platform to be effective.

Orion shifted and flinched. His body ached. His boots were clammy with sweat and the water from broken blisters. His urge to join the fight was strong, but how could he stagger across the battlefield? He considered circling, then hurrying on to Barrel Wells. Fish-hunter might be waiting with Colonel Gater Grey's brigade. Threatened by a possible raid from this beleaguered column, the governor might have believed Sid Peel's story and ordered Federal patrols off the border. Colonel Grey could have slipped through. Safety could lie at Barrel Wells, but how could this column escape from Doc Neston's trap?

Watching from his vantage point, Orion Tibbs waited. He was thankful for the warming sun. He dozed and awoke to the crunch of iron-rimmed wheels. The sun had reached its zenith, and there were long hours to wait until nightfall. He flicked a look toward the twin buttes. The guns were still positioned. Captain Murphy's column lay in their tight circle. Doc Neston's men, with pickets out, had regrouped to a safe distance. Orion crept across his sandy perch and looked back.

Doc Neston's cookwagon, which Orion had last seen on the Crater Pass road, was passing below. The cook, huddling on the spring seat, stared morosely ahead. Orion let it pass, then slid down the sand bank. Limping into a trot, he caught the tailgate and scrambled up. Seconds later he had the muzzle of his Colt peeking through the canvas and pressed against the driver's neck. "Just drive right on, Cookie," Orion ordered. "Put it right between those twin buttes, understand?"

The cook complained, "Them Rebs got howitzers set up there. They'll blow this rig sky-high!"

"Maybe not," said Orion. "Let's just go on up there and find out!"

The minutes dragged. Peeking through the slit

in the canvas, Orion could see that Doc Neston was sending a man out. The horseman waved, signaling the cook to turn. Orion pressed the barrel firmly, and the cook, muttering profanities, ignored the approaching rider.

"Turn off, you blasted fool!" the rider shouted. He waited a few seconds, then, with a worried glance at the howitzer's position, dashed forward.

Orion allowed him to come close enough to ride alongside. "We got the Rebels pinned down up ahead, but they got mountain guns on those buttes!" The rider glared at the sweating cook.

Orion leaned out and the bounty hunter went for his gun. Orion shot him out of the saddle. Then, without hesitation, he lifted the cook by his suspenders and shoved him off the wagon. He caught the reins and shouted at the team. As the tugs tightened, Orion let out another yell. The gate was ahead and the team passed between the buttes. Orion stood up in the seat well, hoping the gunners wouldn't close the gate with a howitzer volley.

"Four dead, ten more wounded, and all exhausted." Captain Murphy, his shoulders sagging, squatted behind the wagon and finished his report. The column, Orion learned, had marched through the last day and a full night. They had spotted Neston's posse with just time enough to hoist the howitzers onto the two buttes.

"Can you get those howitzers off?" Orion asked.

Captain Murphy nodded. "They're within our handgun range. If Neston tries to close in, we can kill more than he can stand to lose." He brightened. "Now that you've brought in that wagon, we've got a gun platform. Mounted, those howitzers can keep riflemen back out of range. Our walking cavalry"—he smiled at Orion—"can hold back any mounted charge." He frowned and added, "Until dark, but after that?" He shook his head.

"It figures," agreed Orion. "We've still got about three hours of daylight. At Barrel Wells we can hole in. It'd take the whole Federal army to dig us out of there."

Almost gleeful with relief, Captain Murphy laughed. "You talk like a damned Reb!" He rose and stepped away from the wagon, stretched to his full height, and began to issue orders.

"Lieutenant Hinds, have this wagon stripped right down to the sideboards. Send out a squad of twenty men to assist Sergeant Rosser. I want those guns off the sand piles and mounted on this wagon in exactly ten minutes. Now, Lieutenant" —he gazed straight into the eyes of the young blond officer—"pick fifty men and feint a charge on that bounty-hunter camp. Hold your positions until you see this wagon leave, then withdraw slowly. We'll provide cover fire with the howitzers. Understand?" The lieutenant grinned, and every man within earshot grinned with him.

"Now," Captain Murphy snapped, "hop to it, soldiers!"

19

Throughout the dragging afternoon death rode
alongside the guerrilla column. Captain Murphy
maneuvered his forces as if the column were a
giant spring. The howitzers, mounted on the
wagon bed, stayed in the center of the march. A
shot now and then kept Doc Neston's riders out of
rifle range. The Rebels, with bleak eyes, hollow
faces, and very tired bodies, moved with grim de-
termination toward Barrel Wells.

Doc Neston's men slashed at all sides of the column. The Texas bounty hunters had come a long
way to collect. Their prize, like some giant cater-
pillar, was edging toward safety. The man hunters
knew, once the guerrillas were protected by the
rock ridges, they would be impossible to over-
come. It had to be now. Small groups of horsemen
made endless forays. Each time they were beaten
back, but at a cost to Murphy's limited ammunition.

Orion Tibbs, leading the team, kept the wagon
in the exact center of the struggling column. He

admired the stamina of these Missouri soldiers. Without sleep, on short rations, and without horses, they had crossed most of Arizona. Except for the cannon and an occasional revolver burst when a horse came in too close, these men had held their fire. Orion was also aware that the Neston crew, particularly the horses, were tiring. The bounty hunters had moved swiftly, and except for the one night spent on Crater Pass, had moved day and night.

With darkness only an hour away, Sergeant Rosser shouted from the gun position, "Captain Murphy, sir?"

"Yes, Sergeant?" The officer hurried up and Orion joined them.

The sergeant lowered his voice. "Sorry to report, sir, but we're down to our last four rounds."

Captain Murphy turned to Tibbs. "Marshal, how far are we from Barrel Wells?"

"Top this rise and it's less than half a mile," Orion replied. "You'd better save those last rounds. Doc Neston's been moving his men on ahead. He could be figuring to hold you off until dark, then ride us down."

"There's no effective cover here." Captain Murphy studied the area. Low-lying mesquite were bunched between rocks lying on the slope.

Ancient rocks that would crumble if stacked for defense. "Does this hill drop into Barrel Wells, Marshal?"

"Just top the rise and it's all downhill, Captain," explained Orion. "It's a deep pool with rock ledges on three sides."

"Sandstone?"

"Mostly. Some boulders and the usual dunes that move around with the wind."

The captain was calm. "Sandstone can't stand up under cannon fire. Let Neston's men get into those caves . . ." He smiled faintly. "We've still got four rounds. We'll spray those ledges with canister and send in a clean-up squad. Neston's men will come out!"

Orion wasn't so sure. Riflemen, sniping among those rocks, could pour in a terrible crossfire. The guerrillas would have to sustain a charge on foot. If they hesitated, halted just once, Doc Neston's crew would cut them to pieces.

"Lieutenant!" Captain Murphy's command brought Hinds forward on the double. "The men are to discard packs. Load all hand weapons."

Hinds barked orders as Orion watched. Each pack held four to six navy revolvers. Each handgun had a lanyard cord approximately two feet long. The men draped the cords over their shoulders and stuffed spare cylinders into handy pockets.

Captain Murphy's pride was evident. "Real guerrilla firepower, Marshal. Developed by Quantrill back in Missouri. Sabers and carbines are useful when army fights army, but for hit-and-run you can't beat handguns." He swelled his chest and clinched both fists. "Today Doc Neston and his bounty men are going to learn a lesson!"

Lieutenant Hinds presented himself and barked, "Captain, all men equipped and ready, sir."

"Thank you, Lieutenant." Captain Murphy turned to Sergeant Rosser and ordered, "We'll move to the top. Throw your shells against the rifle pockets. After we engage, take your gun crews and work over the ledges. Roust out survivors." With a small smile he whirled back to Orion. "You're on your own, Marshal."

Orion nodded and returned the sergeant's quizzical grin. They waited, watching the footsore guerrillas reach the top of the slope. With a nod to his crew, Sergeant Rosser slapped the horses and the gun wagon moved upward.

The captain was leading his men. The lines were ragged, but each man kept abreast of his partner. They moved down the slope solemnly.

Some staggered and slipped to their knees but were hoisted to their feet and stayed in line.

There was a lull in the gunfire. This was no surprise to Neston's men. They were just waiting for the guerrillas to reach perfect rifle range. Below, the water—a willow-edged pond in a horseshoe of rock—caught the setting sun and glowed with a dozen colors. The dunes, once tall, had been flattened by the wind.

The rifle fire of the defenders was beginning. Slugs sang out from the ledges. Neston's horsemen, gathered in a line, formed a barrier between the column and the water. The horsemen now joined the firing. The gap was narrowing. A guerrilla stumbled and slumped slowly to the sand.

Behind him Orion heard Sergeant Rosser growl. The team was swung, the brakes set, and Rosser lowered the muzzle of one howitzer. He touched off a fuse. The weapon thumped. Seconds later it exploded against the top of the ledge and showered rock fragments over the line of horsemen. The horses squealed. Rosser reloaded, ignited, and again the rocks flew. Bounty hunters scrambled out of the protective holes and scampered off the ledges. The horsemen fought to control the excited animals. The wagon team reared, lifting Orion off his feet. The wagon bed tilted as Rosser got off the third round.

Doc Neston rode in to whip his horsemen back into line. But now the guerrillas were rolling on, closing to handgun range. Captain Murphy still led, and weary skirmishers tried to keep up with him.

Sergeant Rosser lighted the last fuse and leaped from the gun platform. The howitzer banged as the gun crew sped to catch up with the sergeant. Below, the skirmishers had halted.

Orion Tibbs swore. So close to victory, or at least the safety of Barrel Wells, were the guerrillas quitting? He could no longer see the captain. Several guerrillas opened fire, but they were still out of effective range. Doc Neston had regrouped his horsemen, and the tempo of their carbines picked up.

Sergeant Rosser's squad had reached the rim of the nearest ledge. Orion, ready to follow, paused. Below, the men had gathered around the captain, who was wounded, and the charge was stalled. A hundred yards short of the pond, and only a few steps more were needed to bring Neston's men into the range of those lethal navy Colts.

Orion hooked a hand onto the hames of the near horse, swung aboard, and lashed the team down the sandy slope. The wagon bounced and dislodged the howitzers. The horses frantically outran the leaping wagon. Like a chariot with its

tail on fire, Orion's runaway rig caught up with
the guerrillas' line. Moving aside, they flowed in
behind and found the strength to trot.

Doc Neston saw it coming and broke away from
his horsemen. Riding low, he threw lead at Orion.
Delaying to the final moment, Orion grasped the
animal's bridle and yanked. The frantic team
swung and the wagon flipped.

As the tugs broke, Orion hung on. The animals
staggered free of the careening wagon. Orion
watched, breathless. The wagon tipped, began to
flip, and crashed into Doc Neston. It rolled over
and Orion could see Neston tangled in the spin-
ning wheels.

Behind him the guerrillas had reached their
gun range. Revolver fire barked like keening
dogs, and wild rebel yells sang out over the fight.
It was man for man now. Guerrillas yanked
bounty hunters out of their saddles, and combat-
ants struggled together in the deep sand.

On the higher ledge Sergeant Rosser's squad
had opened up. Doc Neston's riflemen, caught in
the pocket at the base of the rocks, left their scant
cover. The guerrilla skirmishers were still head-
hunting along the Neston line of horses.

"Break through! Break through!" Captain
Murphy had gained his feet and was staggering
through the melee. His skirmishers followed and

met the riflemen head-on. The handguns roared like giant firecrackers and dropped the riflemen to the sandy floor. The guerrilla column, like an infuriated scorpion, smashed ahead and sidled into the safety of the dunes surrounding Barrel Wells.

Orion Tibbs swung his tiring team and raced across the battlefield. Most of the column had broken through. Some were already sprawled in defensive positions, reloading their iron. Captain Murphy, limping, was clambering onto the top of a flattened sand dune. Leaping off the frothing horse, Orion joined the captain.

"It was absolutely magnificent!" the captain shouted. He looked up at the top of the ledge and again raised his voice. "Sergeant, take prisoners!" He scanned the rocks and rapped out another order. "Lieutenant, send out a detail to corral those horses! Then send a company out to bring in the howitzers."

The battle was over. Wounded men lay along the route taken by the runaway howitzer wagon. Its flailing wheels had cut slashes in the soft ground. Doc Neston was a crumpled lump, and his crew of bounty hunters had scattered. There was no doubt who had won. For a time, a short time at least, this column of Missouri rebels could rest.

"Captain Murphy, sir." Sergeant Rosser had located a horse and ridden it back onto the higher ridge. He was pointing south. "Horsemen approaching, Captain." He peered into the falling darkness and added, "Can't say for sure, Captain, but it sort of looks like the brigade!"

20

It *was* the brigade. Five hundred well-mounted guerrilla fighters followed Colonel Gater Grey into Barrel Wells. Captain Murphy's column, exuberant with victory, broke into the ranks to greet relatives and comrades. Fish-hunter, wearing faint worry lines around his eyes, smiled when he finally located Marshal Orion Tibbs.

Captain Murphy conferred with his colonel. In the next ten minutes squads were assigned to bury the dead, care for the wounded, and hunt down Doc Neston's surviving bounty hunters. The new arrivals from Mexico, fresh and well armed, quickly scattered over the rise. Before the hour had passed, the brigade's own supply wagons, high-wheeled ambulances, rattled in. Fires were lighted, and the smell of roasting beef swept over the camp at Barrel Wells.

Orion Tibbs had a short meeting with Colonel Grey and Captain Murphy. The colonel was a tiger of a man. All lean muscle, taut skin exposing the cheekbones, and close-cropped graying hair.

His comments were brief and his decisions abrupt.

"Captain Murphy has reported on your splendid behavior, Marshal Tibbs. Your courage and assistance will be long remembered by this brigade. When its history is compiled, there will be space for the gallant men, afoot in this unfriendly land, who reached safety by the combined efforts of a pair of howitzers and the aid of the sheriff of Pineville." The colonel, obviously elated at this belated rescue of his rear guard, paused to seek the right words. His voice, mellow with appreciation, savored his next words. "Moreover, Marshal, all those who benefited from your courage and your unselfish aid will forever honor you in their hearts!"

"Thank you," Orion answered. "Fish-hunter and I will be drifting back to Prescott. There's a Judge Yontz who may need some support."

"It would be our pleasure, Marshal," replied Colonel Grey, "to march on Prescott and—"

"Oh, no, no, Colonel," Orion said hastily. "All Yontz really needs are some logic and facts and to get pointed in the right direction. He's a holy terror." He watched the colonel's face fall and quickly added, "I'm sure the border patrols have been pulled back into Prescott. Your return to Mexico should be . . ."

"Accelerated?" Colonel Grey sounded disappointed. "Of course you're right, Marshal. You get on back and take care of that carpetbagging governor." He smiled sadly. "If the North had more like *him*, the South would have won the war."

"Perhaps the marshal will accept an escort?" offered Captain Murphy. "The bounty hunters are well scattered, but they might cause you some trouble."

Orion Tibbs shook his head. "Doc Neston's dead. The rest will cut and run for Texas." After a handshake all around, Fish-hunter and Orion Tibbs rode out.

At a quiet spot near the twin buttes, they dismounted. Orion leaned back against a sandstone rock. The sand was warm, and the rising moon edged its face over the distant mountains. Fish-hunter hobbled the horses and walked over to study the marshal. Tibbs looked gaunt. His boots were worn and cracked. His shoulders sagged, but there was a wry smile on his mouth.

"They said, Marshal, you walked that column all the way from Dixiecity?"

Orion nodded wearily. "Arizona is sure a big place. We must have covered a good half of it." He changed the subject. "What kept you?"

"Mexico is also a big place," Fish-hunter retorted easily. "Since the war ended, many rebels have crossed the border. They wished to join with Maximilian. He refuses to hire units. Instead, he offers land. It's colonies along the border he desires. Colonel Grey was not tempted by land and was trying to link up with General Kirby Smith. I found him at Matamores." He shook his head. "The guerrillas, they are still full of fight. They recrossed the border as soon as I mentioned that you were bringing Captain Murphy's column out of the Tooloons." Fish-hunter halted, peered closer, then stared. Orion Tibbs was sound asleep.

Judge Yontz reined in the team on top of Crater Pass. Below, Pineville squatted like a stray in a field of Kentucky blue grass. The bright sun glittered on the windows of the Palace Hotel. Jeff Glory, spruced up like some New Orleans gambler, lifted a new metal-tipped wooden leg off the splash guard and remarked, "The snow's about melted off."

"If it wasn't," growled the judge, "I was going to leave you stranded right up here." The judge was still as huffy as a victorious fighting cock. He had come out of a free-for-all fight with the governor and belatedly realized that his own part in the escape of the Dixiecity column had been questionable. The marshal had been right; illogical but completely right. The carpetbagging governor had been a crook who had sold a license to Doc Neston and proclaimed an illegal declaration of war against Captain Murphy's men.

Sid Peel and Fish-hunter rode up behind the buckboard and exchanged glances. Sid, his right arm still held tightly in a sling, stared over the valley into the Tooloons. The snow water had cascaded over the crater rim, leaving long shafts of whitened ice against the black rocks. The buffalo ponds sparkled.

Sid looked at Fish-hunter, who was gazing raptly at the view. "Admiring the scenery?" the banty-sized deputy asked. Fish-hunter nodded with appreciation. It would be quiet and peaceful in Pineville.

"The judge is still mad 'cause I loaned his wagon from him," complained Jeff Glory as he calmly lighted a stogie. "You know yourself, Judge," he went on pompously, "for once I done everything right. Hadn't I tried to collect the bounty, and hadn't the governor believed I was part of Doc Neston's gang? If that hadn't'a happened, nobody'd ever knowed the governor was a crook." He filled in the dead silence with more plaintive words. "I'm using that bounty money to rebuild the stables. That's good for Pineville, ain't it?" The judge opened his mouth to reply, then shut it with a snap and continued to sulk.

A few yards behind, Orion Tibbs and Mick trailed along. Mick was frisking, pushing Orion's back with gentle nudges of his whiskery muzzle.

"Don't push," Orion grumbled. "Everyone sure seems in a big hurry to get back home." Suddenly he smiled. Up ahead they were waiting for him and Mick to catch up. They were an odd crew. With the exception of the lugubrious Jeff Glory, the others were stolid. Men of action when action was required, but at the moment all drinking in the sight of home.

Back in Prescott, Yontz *had* been a holy terror. The judge, with Sid Peel's support, had accused the harassed governor of breaking every law of man and morality. The governor, wilting, had collected Fred Wade and hightailed it for Texas.

Orion sighed with relief as he mounted Mick. It was all over. Captain Murphy's men were safe in Mexico. Dixiecity was gone, soon to crumble into a weathered pile of blackened beams. Doc Neston was dead. Wesley Neston was buried in the Pineville Cemetery alongside of Max Rosser. The bounty hunters had dispersed. Law, such as it was, had returned to the Tooloon country.

Pressing his knees forward, Orion brought Mick

up alongside his waiting companions. He caught the judge's doleful eye and spoke. "Come on. Let's all get on down into Pineville and see what's busted loose since we've been gone!"

P